SWEET REMEMBRANCE

CHARLESTON HARBOR NOVELS

DEBBIE WHITE

ISBN 9798618598170 KDP PAPERBACK

ISBN - 978-1-7363803-6-9 INGRAM SPARK PAPERBACK

COPYRIGHT @ 2019 Debbie White

This is a work of fiction. Names, characters, organizations, places, events, and incidents are products of the author's imagination or are used fictitiously. Any resemblance to actual persons, living or dead, or actual events is purely coincidental.

Editing by Kerry Genova, writersresourceinc.com

Leo Bricker of The Grammatical Eye®

Cover Design by Larry White

Debbie White Books

Summerville, South Carolina

𝒶 Walk Down Memory Lane

So much has happened over the past few years. One thing is certain, everyone has grown older. Grandmother Lilly and Auntie Patty, despite being in their eighties, kept sisters Annie and Mary constantly on their feet, trying to figure out their moves in advance. But that's what was so enchanting about them. They were youthful, fun to be around, engaging, and always feisty. Maybe that was their secret to longevity.

As thankful as Annie and Mary were to have both Grandmother and Auntie in their corner, they were just as happy to have married into the Powell family where there was no shortage of fun and quirky relatives, too. Milly and Robert were the head of the Powell family, and Annie often said Jack was a wonderful blend of his two parents.

Annie wasn't sure about Mary and Jack's cousin, Danny, being a "thing," but it turned out all right. Grandmother and Auntie loved to banter with Jack's grandparents on both sides. It was nice to have some "seasoned" adults in the room, Grandmother would remind everyone from time to time. And so it seems, no matter what has been thrown at them, be it fires, hurricanes, or health issues, this family stuck together.

The homestead, Sweet Magnolia, shortened to Magnolia, became the gathering place for almost every holiday and celebration. Lady Powell, Jack's beloved motorboat, named by Annie while they were dating, still brought them hours of enjoyment out on the intercoastal waterways. Even Grandmother and Auntie enjoyed boat rides.

When Vicky and Scott moved in on the island and became their neighbors, Annie and Jack didn't feel quite so isolated any longer, and now that Grandmother and Auntie were settled in the cottage near the main house, Annie could sleep better at night.

And even though they didn't do half as much as they wanted to, getting together with friends and family was what brought them the most happiness. Annie's old college buddies and friends before Jack: Vicky, Cassie, and Jessica, along with their spouses, Scott, Ryan, and Tom, all had families of their own. Everyone rejoiced when Rebecca, one of Annie's first hires at the bakery, now married to Annie's old flame and friend, Dr. Michael Carlisle, gave birth to a beautiful baby girl, Kathryn. But when the news came that Vicky and Scott, who were not able to conceive, adopted a little African American girl, and later a boy from Korea, the circle comprised of friends and family were elated for the Collins'. The circle now felt complete. These friends and their significant others were like family to the Powells and McPhersons, and all of the members wouldn't have it any other way.

Annie, realizing a day would come when the circle would be tested with the passing of their elderly family members, knew that the only way to get through anything remotely like that would be to fall back on their cherished memories. She found comfort in knowing that someday, when Ashton and Carolina were ready, they'd dig up the time capsule Annie and Jack buried under the old magnolia tree, the one that stands so stately to this day, and perhaps, make some memories of their own.

INTRODUCTION

Dear Readers,

I hope with all my heart you enjoy the final book in the Charleston Harbor Novels, Sweet Remembrance. It's been a pleasure bringing the characters back for this fourth installment. Annie, Jack, Grandmother, Auntie, along with all of the extended family are such a joy to write. I've become friends with them as I'm sure you have too. If you haven't read the other books in the series, have no fear! I've written this one as a standalone, and I'm hoping as you walk down memory lane and read about the characters, you'll feel as if you already know them when reading this book. Thank you again for your continued readership and loyalty. Stay up to date with all my news by joining my newsletter. You can find out more

by visiting my website at: https://www.authordeb-
biewhite.com

CHAPTER 1

Shielding her eyes from the bright sun, Annie called out for Jack. He'd normally be at work, but they knew her due date was nearing, and Kiawah was a drive to the local hospital in Mount Pleasant. Feeling the humidity instantly, her clothes began to cling to her, sweat beaded above her brow, and she could feel her mild temperament climb to levels that no one would want to see or hear.

"Ashton, come along. Pick up your feet," she said, almost dragging him.

"Mommy," he said, trying to keep up with her long legs. He almost stumbled when she suddenly stopped, scooping him up in her arms. Huffing and puffing, she trotted down to the dock where Lady Powell was anchored. She could see the top of Jack's hat as he worked on the boat.

"Jack," she yelled.

When they made eye contact, he jumped up and ran toward her.

Thankful she didn't have to scream his name again, and he'd figured out it was time, she handed off Ashton to him and picked up the pace back to the house.

"How far apart are the contractions?" he asked.

"My water broke almost fifteen minutes ago. We have to get to the hospital."

"*Déjà vu*," he said with a lighthearted chuckle.

"It's not funny, Jack. We live so far away from the darn hospital."

"You grab your bag; I'll bring the car around front."

They split at the steps leading up to the house, Jack taking Ashton with him. Annie held the rail and ascended the stairs to the porch. Clearly exhausted from her jaunt to the pier, she maneuvered herself and her large belly down the hall to get her overnight bag. Getting a glimpse of herself in the full-length mirror, her hair wet and slicked down around her face, her clothes rumpled and damp, she shook her head. "How on earth could he love me looking like this?" She tried to blow her bangs up and away, but they were glued to her forehead. Grunting, she picked up her bag and made her way to the porch.

With a harrumph, she plopped down into the front seat and stretched her seat belt. It snapped back into the cover.

"I'm so big the seat belt won't even fit over me," she cried.

Jack leaned over and stretched the belt across her and secured it. He would never admit to her how much strength it took, but she could see it through his gritted teeth.

"Did you let your grandmother and auntie know?" he said as he drove away from the house.

"No! Stop the car!"

Squealing to an abrupt halt, Jack hopped out. He held up a finger as he raced to the front door of the cottage. He rapped twice but no answer. He turned around and grimaced.

"Where are those two?" she mumbled under her breath. She hit the button to the window and poked her head out. "They're not there?"

He tried the doorknob, and the door opened. She could hear him call their names. He stepped inside and was gone for just a minute when he ran back to the car, making her heart drop.

"What? Did something happen?"

"They're not in there. The beds are made, the kitchen is exceptionally clean, but no sign of them."

Annie dropped her head back and moaned.

"I'm sure they're all right."

Annie began to go through her breathing techniques she'd learned at her Lamaze class. "Step on it! I'm going to have a baby," she wailed. "I can't worry about them right now. They're probably at the Black-Eyed Pea drinking Bloody Marys."

Jack punched it as she'd instructed him, and kicking up a bit of gravel and dust, tore out of the homestead, and quickly got them to the main road.

"Daddy, Mommy is hurt," Ashton said.

"No, Mommy isn't hurt. She's having your baby sister."

"Carolina?" Ashton said. "She's coming today?"

"Yes, and I need for you to be a big boy."

Ashton grinned.

Ashton, nearing five years old, had a vocabulary much older thanks to Grandmother Lilly. He knew words like scoundrel, although an outsider might not recognize it, and hooligan came out like hoolandthegang, skedaddle sounded like skittle, drudgery more like judgery, but when he said Praise Jesus, everyone said Amen.

Jack drove as fast as he comfortably could, considering he carried his pregnant wife and young child in the car with him. The stronger the contractions came and the closer in time, the more he felt the need to accelerate, and he did. Not a rule breaker, he constantly checked his rearview mirror for police. Surely, they'd understand.

"Jack, they're coming fast and hard."

"I'm already going ten over the speed limit, Annie." He checked his mirror.

"I feel the need to bear down," she said, now crying.

"Not here, Annie. We're on the darn highway. Give me just five more minutes."

"Tell Carolina that," she moaned at the top of her lungs.

"Daddy," Ashton said.

Jack observed his son's sad face in the rearview mirror.

"I'm scared."

"No reason to be scared, Son. Mommy is in a little discomfort right now."

"Discomfort?" Annie screamed at the top of her lungs.

Jack yelled, "Hold on, Ashton." Then he put the pedal to the metal.

JACK HELD Annie's hand as she went through her breathing exercise. He tried to concentrate on helping her, but with Ashton sitting in the lobby with a nurse, it was hard to give her his full attention.

"Just a few more pushes, Mrs. Powell," the doctor said.

Squeezing Jack's hand as she went through a painful push had him almost screaming out at the same time as she. He remained closed mouthed. No one liked a drama queen. Especially in a guy.

A small cry came at first, followed by a louder one. The nurse swaddled the baby and put her in Annie's arms.

"Here's your beautiful daughter."

Jack kissed Annie on the forehead. "She has your little heart-shaped lips."

"And my red hair." Annie began to choke up with emotion.

"We have to wait for her eyes to turn their true color, but I'm betting they'll be green." Jack winked at Annie, making her flash a wide grin.

"Let me go weigh her and get all the pertinent information. I'll have her back in no time. By the way, what did you name her?" The nurse removed the baby from Annie's arms.

"Carolina," they both said in unison.

"Carolina," the nurse repeated.

"Carolina Margaret Powell," Annie said, her eyes misting as she fell in love with her daughter.

"How are you feeling, dear?" Jack held her hand firmly.

"Like I just had a baby. I wonder how much she weighs. She wasn't as easy as Ashton."

"Maybe she'll have a small stubborn streak?" His eyes twinkled with humor.

"Stubborn streak. Like me?" She blinked her eyes.

Jack measured a little with his thumb and index finger. "A tad."

"Guilty. I suppose. Where's Ashton?"

"Oh! I almost forgot. He's in the waiting room with a nice nurse."

"Don't forget to call the family," she yelled as he exited the room.

Shaking her head, she giggled to herself and then scowled. She felt pretty good, but she did just give birth. Letting her head sink into the pillow, she closed her eyes, taking a small catnap. She'd only had them shut for a few seconds when Jack brought Ashton in.

"There's my big boy," she said, propping herself up on the pillow, trying not to make a bunch of faces and scare Ashton.

"Mommy, is Carolina here? I want to play with her."

Annie looked up at Jack. Her gaze traveled down to Ashton. "Honey, Carolina is too little to play with right now. She's going to do a lot of sleeping when we first get home."

"After she wakes up," he said.

The nurse came in with Carolina and put her back in Annie's arms. "Eight pounds four ounces and twenty-one inches long."

"She's the same length as Ashton, but a bit chunkier," Annie said, staring at the sleeping bundle.

"Why don't you try and nurse her. We'll give you some privacy." The nurse placed her hand in Ashton's and started to leave.

"Wait," Annie called. "Ashton hasn't met his little sister yet."

The nurse smiled.

Jack picked up Ashton and sat him on the bed next to his mom. Annie took one of his little hands and moved it over Carolina's arm. "Isn't she soft?"

He nodded.

"This is Carolina Margaret. Your baby sister. For you to love and protect, Ashton." Jack rested his hand on Ashton's shoulder.

"I will protect her from all hoolandthegangs."

Annie tipped her head. "I'm sure you will, Son. I'm sure you will."

"I'm going to step out into the lobby and finish up calling everyone."

"Did you get hold of Grandmother and Auntie?"

Jack shook his head. "I called them first. No answer."

"Try them again. I'm so worried about them. Where in the world could they have gone?"

"You let me worry about them. I'll find out what they've been up to."

"Knowing them, Jack, no good." Annie began to feed Carolina.

Jack ducked out of the room with Ashton so Annie could nurse in peace. He tried the cottage phone again, their cell, and when he still couldn't reach Lilly or Patty, he finished up the calls to others, letting them know about Carolina. After about twenty minutes of answering all the same questions, he sat staring at the television in the lobby, tossing his phone around in the palm of his hands.

JACK SAW THEM COME IN. Two uniformed police searching the waiting room for their caller. He stood and waved. "Hi. I'm Jack Powell. I called you about my wife's grandmother and auntie."

"Can you give us a description of them," the shorter policeman with a round, balding spot on his head said.

"Grandmother Lilly and Auntie Patty are eighty. They're in pretty good shape. They don't drive, so they had to get a lift to wherever it is they are. Grandmother has silver hair, walks with a cane, and usually is dressed as if she were going to the queen's for tea."

The police officer looked up and smiled.

"Auntie Patty is a bit less flamboyant. She has silver-streaked hair, walks with a slight limp, and also dresses rather formally. They're sisters, and Patty is the youngest by about fifteen months."

"And they were last seen at your house on Kiawah?" the officer with a round face asked.

"At the cottage on our property. We're right off Marsh Boulevard, near the lagoon. Sweet Magnolia sets back from the water about five hundred yards or so."

"Sweet Magnolia?" the bald officer asked.

Jack chuckled. "That's what we named the place. See my wife, Annie, owns Sweet Indulgence in Charleston, then we have the home, Sweet Magnolia and my wood business, Powell's Sweet Wood Design."

"And your boy here. Is his name Sweet something or other?" Both officers broke out in laughter.

"No. This is Ashton," Jack said, perturbed they'd made fun of his and Annie's play on words.

"Okay, so we have the descriptions and the last place they were seen. What time was it you last saw them?" The bald officer quirked a brow.

"Well," Jack stammered. "I actually didn't see them

today at all."

"And your wife?" the other officer asked.

"I'm not sure. I'll need to ask her. She just gave birth to our second child. A girl. Carolina Margaret." Jack rolled up on the ball of his foot and slowly eased back down, smiling ear to ear.

"Congratulations. We'll be right back." The two officers exited the hospital.

Jack kept an eye on them as they talked on the radio and then chatted with each other. He wondered what they were saying. After about ten minutes, they came back in.

"So, looks like they've been found," the officer said.

"Safe? I mean, they weren't hurt or anything?" Jack asked.

"They took an Uber to a movie, apparently. Said they wanted to see Downton Abbey," the officer with the bald head said.

"Downton Abbey!" Jack whirled around and stared at the waiting room. He slowly turned back around to face the officers. "I apologize for reporting them missing. It's just they're eighty, and when we couldn't get in touch with them, we feared the worst."

"No apology necessary. They're on their way back to the cottage and will wait for you there."

The officers left, and Jack slumped to the chair.

"Daddy, what's wrong?"

He'd almost forgotten he had Ashton with him. He'd been so quiet.

"Nothing, hon. Grandmother Lilly and Auntie Patty went to the movies and didn't tell anyone they were going. When I had to bring Mommy to the hospital, I tried to let them know where we were going. It's always a good idea to tell someone where you are." He lifted Ashton's chin with a finger. "You'll always let us know where you're going, right?"

"Of course, Daddy."

Jack nodded. His Ashton was a big boy, indeed. Tall for his age, and developing a vocabulary suited for a ten-year-old, Ashton Robert Powell had it going on. Jack chuckled then patted Ashton on the knee. "Let's go tell Mommy Grandmother and Auntie have been found."

Jack poked his head around the drapery. "Can we come in?" he whispered.

"The nurse just came and got her. She ate quite a bit. She's a feisty little one. I can see already she's different than Ashton." Her gaze floated to her boy.

"Grandmother and Auntie went to the movies without telling anyone," Ashton blurted.

Annie lifted her gaze to meet Jack's.

"It's true. I called in a missing person's report. They were discovered leaving the theater here in Mount Pleasant."

"Mount Pleasant! Gah! Those two. How'd they get there? Mary?"

"Uber," Ashton belted.

Annie lowered her gaze to him. "Let Daddy tell me."

"Uber," Jack whispered as he tipped his head.

Shaking her head, she balled her hand and hit the mattress. "I'll handle this later. As long as they're safe. I presume they're headed home?"

"Yes. That's what the officer said."

"Please call Vicky and see if she can meet them at the cottage and sit with them until you get there."

"Will do. Why don't you try and get some rest? I'll be here bright and early to pick up my favorite girls." He leaned over and kissed Annie on the cheek.

"Ashton." Annie opened her arms.

Jack swooped down and picked him up and placed him in Annie's arms.

"I love you, Ashton. Be a good boy for Daddy, and Carolina and I will see you tomorrow." She gave him a peck on the nose then the lips.

"Yes, Mommy."

Jack set Ashton down and held his hand. "See you tomorrow." He blew her a kiss.

Mouthing *I love you*, she dropped her head back to the pillow and closed her eyes.

CHAPTER 2

Once Annie had gotten home from the hospital, she was determined to do things differently with Carolina. She let her cry a little bit longer, didn't jump up the minute she fussed, maybe even left the diaper on just a tad longer. Well, at least five seconds longer. She didn't worry about the daily bath but instead wiped her down from top to bottom several times throughout the day, and when Ashton asked if he could hold her, she let him sit on the couch with Carolina's little head resting on his lap, supervising to ensure he didn't do anything too boyish, like jumping off quickly and letting Carolina roll off.

Even though Jack was on paternity leave, people were asking for furniture pieces along with custom signs for when he returned. After checking in on the business side of things, he shared with Annie his doubts he'd be able to complete all the orders without help. She took in a deep breath and laid out a new business plan for him. After all, she opened Sweet Indulgence and had some experience in running a business. Although, she'd not stepped inside the well-known bakery for a while. The last time she did, she felt out of place. As if she didn't belong there anymore. Hogwash, she said under her breath as she scribbled out Jack's new plan. "Sweet Indulgence will always be mine."

"Huh?" Jack asked with a puzzled look.

"Oh, I just was confirming that Sweet Indulgence is my baby and always will be."

"Why would you think she wasn't? Your baby," he said.

"The last time I entered the bakery, everyone was working so hard, things looked great, and I didn't think they missed me." Annie held Carolina in the crux of her arm while she sat at the table, watching Carolina's chest rise and fall as she slept.

"I know that's not true. They're just carrying on like you trained them." He reached over and touched her arm.

"I guess. But then there is a part of me that might not mind giving up control." She fidgeted with her hair.

He tilted his head. "You'd sell the cupcakery?"

"I don't know if I'd sell it, but maybe just step back."

"That's what you've done, Annie. Selling it would be the next step if that's what you want to do. But I'm in no way suggesting you do that. I know you started that place from the ground up, worked it by yourself until you began earning money, hiring employees, training them, and the fire…that was awful." He hung his head.

"I have two children and an aging grandmother and auntie who need me. Not to mention a handsome and understanding husband."

He leaned forward, kissing her on the mouth. "The kids will be fine with whatever you decide, Annie."

"Grandmother and Auntie?"

"Right now, those two are doing great. I know you've had some concern regarding their health, but seems their medication is working well. I mean, they take off without telling anyone where they go. They're pretty independent."

"I had a long talk with them about their last episode. Going to the movies to see Downton Abbey!"

"It was a great movie," Jack said, nodding.

Annie cut him a warning look.

Shrugging, he laughed. "Well, it was." He flashed a snowy-white grin.

"I had a message from Mary. Something about the house. Did Danny say anything to you about it?"

Pushing his chair back, Jack stood and stretched.

Annie watched as he refused to make eye contact with her. "Jack?"

"Yes, dear?" He stooped over and picked up Carolina, rocking her gently in his arms.

"Do you know something about the house you're not telling me?"

"Oh, I think she's had a blowout." He lifted his hand, showing Annie the yellowish stuff.

Jack rushed down the hall to change Carolina. He knew something. It was just perfect timing Carolina required a diaper change. Thumping her fingers on the table, she looked over at the cell phone lying nearby. Whenever it came to Mary, something was always up. She picked up the phone and called her.

"What's up, Sis?"

"Hey. How's Carolina?"

"She's doing well. We're going to make her one tough cookie," Annie said, laughing at their slack parenting job.

"And Ashton?"

"Yup, he's doing good."

"No jealousy rearing its ugly head?" Mary said.

"Not yet. But we're trying to include him in many

things. And there's not the age difference like existed between you and me."

"True. Well, glad everything is going well."

A long pause entered the conversation.

"I was thinking about doing some refreshing here at the house. Do you have any problem with that?" Mary asked.

Annie, shaking her head, replied, "No."

"I just hate the wallpaper in the living room and the dining room. It's so old-world looking."

"Old-world looking? The house is pretty old, Mary. Grandmother decorated it according to the style of the home and where it's located. What were you thinking?"

"I don't know. Maybe some bold paint colors. I just can't have the monkey wallpaper any longer," Mary said.

Annie chuckled into the phone. She knew exactly what Mary meant. Grandmother fell in love with the almost jungle-themed paper. Tigers and monkeys hanging from tree limbs, it was supposed to be whimsical with tones of European adventure. But truth be told, Annie didn't care for it all that much either.

"I don't know, Mary. Maybe find out how attached Grandmother is to the paper first. I agree it's a tad over- whelming, but it definitely speaks to Grandmother. It's right up her alley. What colors were you thinking?"

Jack entered the room, carrying Carolina. Annie

nodded to him as she mouthed Mary's name. He tiptoed out of the room, giving her privacy.

"I have a few samples. Would you be able to come by and look?"

"Sure. I'm ready to get out of the house. The walls are caving in."

"So happy to hear that, Annie."

Annie knew what Mary was referring to. With Ashton, she couldn't bear to leave him or the house. But things were different this time around.

No sooner had her phone call ended with Mary, Grandmother Lilly and Auntie Patty came busting through the door. Arguing.

"I don't need you to help me walk, Patty!" Lilly fumed.

"You were a bit unsteady out there, Lilly. I was just trying to be helpful," Patty said.

"What's wrong with you two now?" Annie walked over to them, taking Lilly's arm.

"Oh, that sister of mine. She's always behaving like my mother. I don't need a mother. I'm older than she." She sat down in the chair Annie scooted out for her.

"You do seem a little unsteady on your feet. Did you check your blood sugar this morning?" Annie crossed her arms while tapping her toes.

"No, she didn't. But I'm happy to report mine is good. 102." Patty's boasted tone hit a nerve with Lilly.

"Tattletale." Lilly stuck her tongue out.

"Can I get either of you a glass of iced tea?" Annie moved to the kitchen.

"Yes, dear. It's brutally hot and humid outside today," Patty said, sitting next to Lilly.

"Where are the children?" Lilly asked.

"Jack has Carolina and Ashton. They're upstairs in the playroom."

"He's such a sweetheart," Patty said.

Annie joined her relatives at the table. "Wondered if you two would like to go with me to the house. Mary wants to do some decorating and would like our blessing."

Lilly grumbled while shaking her head. "Decorating? There's nothing wrong with the place. What in the world is she up to, Annie?"

"She just wants to refresh the décor."

"She is living in the house, Lilly," Patty said, chiming in.

"That may be true, but it is still our property. We are the landlords. Everything must be run through us. Everything." She slammed the palm of her hand on the table.

"And that's why I'm asking you to go with me, Grandmother," Annie said, trying to hide her irritation.

"Knowing Mary, she'll want to tear down my wall-paper that I had shipped over from Europe and paint the walls purple!" Lilly took a drink of her iced tea.

Annie tried to refrain from giving away any knowledge she had regarding décor changes. She raised her brows and drew in a sip of the iced tea. Should she say something? Anything? Naw. Let Mary be the one.

"So, how about we go out there this afternoon. I need to shower and get dressed. Mary wants to see Carolina too. I'll see if Ashton can stay here with Jack. Not sure I'm ready to handle two small ones out in the world just yet."

The two old ladies slid back their chairs at almost the exact time. "We'll be ready," Lilly said, standing then quickly grabbing the chair back.

"Jack," Annie yelled up the stairs.

Jack appeared at the landing.

"I need to walk Grandmother and Auntie back over to the cottage. I'll be back in ten minutes."

"Hello, Lilly and Patty," Jack called.

"Hello, dear Jack," Lilly answered. "I see you have your hands full." She chuckled.

Patty held up her hand and waved. "Nice to see you, Jack."

Annie laced her arm with Lilly and took Patty by the hand.

"Is this necessary?" Lilly scowled.

"Yes. And as soon as we get to the cottage, you're taking your blood sugar."

"YOUR NUMBERS ARE HIGH, Grandmother. Are you taking your medication as prescribed?" Annie moved to the cabinet and retrieved Grandmother's pills, unscrewing the cap off and peering inside.

"Yes, I took it," Grandmother said.

"She's not eating properly," Patty blurted.

Annie twisted her face in a puzzling look. "How can that be? You eat dinner with us every night. I make sure both of you are eating fewer carbs and more vegetables and lean meat."

"She eats a donut for breakfast, and potato chips for lunch," Patty said, rushing toward another cabinet.

Annie walked over to the shelf and removed a box of donuts and a bag of chips. Holding them, she scowled at Lilly. "You couldn't even have the good taste to buy decent donuts? These are store-bought. And how did you get them?"

"I'm not a prisoner, Annie."

"Of course not, Grandmother. But seriously. If you want some baked goods, at least let me make some or take you to a nice bakery. These are full of hydrogenated oil and high fructose. Yuck." Annie tossed the items onto the counter.

"I'll be back over to get you in about an hour. Let's go out to lunch before we head over to Mary's."

"Can Jack handle the children for that length of time?" Patty asked.

Annie swiped the air with her hand. "Sure. He can handle anything. He's Jack Powell."

CHAPTER 3

"**I** have my phone," Annie said, holding it up. "Call me if you need me to come home. I just fed Carolina so she'll be good for two hours. After that, give her one of the bottles—"

"Honey, I got it. This isn't my first rodeo." Jack put his arm around her shoulders and gently directed her toward the front door. "You women have a great time together. We'll be fine." He dropped a kiss on her forehead.

"Thank you, Jack."

"For what?" He cocked his head.

"For being the best husband and father in the entire world."

He puffed out his chest and smiled.

Leaving the children with Jack, Annie drove over to

the cottage. Quickly running up to the porch, she knocked twice. She turned the handle and popped her head inside. "Grandmother. Auntie. I'm out front."

"Coming, dear," Patty called out.

Annie stepped back out and waited for them. She tried to give them as much privacy and independence as possible, but because Grandmother was behaving strangely that morning, she stood by to help them down the stairs.

Dressed like they were going to a gala event, Grandmother wore a two-piece pant set in peacock blue, pearls around her neck and on her ears, and her hair piled high on her head with a silvery rhinestone clip. Auntie wore a yellow two-piece outfit and black pearls, leaving her hair down with soft curls resting on her shoulders. These two women knew how to live and definitely knew how to dress. Annie looked down at her maternity top and capris with her white Keds that had seen better days. She tugged on her ponytail, then let her fingers drop to her ears where her lobes were free of any jewelry.

"You both look lovely," Annie said.

Grandmother's gaze dropped to Annie's shoes.

"I know. I'm not looking as put together as you all. But I did just have a baby." She took Grandmother by the hand and led her down the steps, with Patty holding on to the railing, coming down on her own.

"Take it easy, ladies," Annie said, helping them to the car.

"Annie McPherson-Powell. You treat us like children," Lilly said.

The ride to downtown was lively. Grandmother and Patty kept Annie entertained. They went into more detail about their recent trip to Mount Pleasant, where they saw the movie and stopped at the store to get junk food. Annie discovered that it wasn't the first time they'd snuck out without telling them.

"If you must know, we've done it a few times," Patty admitted.

"How do I not know that?" Annie glared at Patty in the rearview mirror.

"When you'd go to your doctor appointments, we would sneak out. We've been to see Rebecca's grandmother, Ethel, we've seen a couple of movies, and we've even been out to lunch," Lilly said.

"I don't mind taking you anywhere you'd like to go. We just have to schedule it," Annie said.

"That's the thing. We're not used to being on someone's schedule," Lilly said.

"Grandmother, you knew when you moved to the cottage that things would be different. We live a few miles from town, in case you hadn't noticed. We have to schedule things," Annie said.

"Not with Uber," Patty said, smiling.

Annie shot her a death stare "Uber? You'd rather take a ride from a stranger than from me or Jack...or Mary even?"

"We've met some very nice people during our rides. You'd be surprised," Patty said, nodding.

"Okay, guys. Let's change the subject, shall we? I will just say one more thing. Please, please let us know when you're going out. We worry about you. And when I went into labor and couldn't reach you, I got scared. That only added to my stress of giving birth."

"I'm hungry," Lilly said.

Annie shook her head and tried to conceal her grin. These two old women were a hoot. And if they ever knew the family admired their spunk, fortitude, and energy, they'd have a lot more to worry about than the occasional trip into town to see a movie.

"One of the drivers told us she'd been ziplining. It sounded interesting," Patty said.

Annie grimaced.

After a lunch of fried flounder, hush puppies, and a slice of cheesecake they all shared, they headed to the house to visit with Mary.

"Grandmother! Auntie! So nice to see you both," Mary said, opening her arms.

Grandmother leaned in, brushing her lips across her

cheek. Patty hugged her tightly, kissing her on the mouth.

"Hey, Sis," Mary said.

Annie flopped up her hand. "Hey."

"You look good," she said.

"I do not. You don't have to sugarcoat it, Sis. I look frumpy and fat."

"No, you do not. Besides. You just gave birth."

"Whatever," Annie said, waving her off. We're here to see your color palate for the refresh."

"Yes. I can't wait to see what you've chosen," Grandmother sneered.

The four of them sauntered into the living room. Grandmother gasped. "My wallpaper. What have you done?"

Annie's gaze flew up to the wall.

"I took down some of the paper so we can see how the paint will look," Mary said.

Grandmother ran her hand along the wall. "This wallpaper was very expensive. I had it special ordered. From Europe."

Annie could hear the hurt in her grandmother's voice.

"I asked Annie what she thought about me tearing it down."

"I never said you should tear it down. I told you to discuss it with them first. Show us your ideas. That's what I said. If you heard something else, Mary, then that's on you."

The two-foot by six-foot section, now minus wallpaper, had several brushstrokes of varying paint colors.

Patty, who had been quiet up to that moment, stepped forward. "This is pretty," she said, admiring the eggplant color.

"No! That's awful," Grandmother said, spewing spittle as she spoke, clearly agitated with Mary.

"Maybe this color would be nice," Annie said, pointing to the celery sample.

Grandmother grunted.

"That's nice too," Patty said.

"You can never just leave well enough alone, can you Mary McPherson." Grandmother tapped her cane a few times then moved away from the wall, looking around the room. "What happened to the chintz upholstered chairs?" She raised her brows to match her elevated tone.

"Those old things? I donated them." Mary, sounding pleased by her generosity, soon was lambasted by Grandmother.

"Donated? You donated the chairs that had been in this room for over fifty years?"

"Mary! Why didn't you just recover them if you hated the pattern so much? You had no right to just give away

Grandmother's and Auntie's furnishings." Annie crossed her arms and stared at her sister.

"You said this was Danny's and mine. We could make it comfortable. That's what we are doing. Now you're taking it all back. That's it. I didn't want to live in the old drafty house anyway. I did it for you." She whirled around and rushed toward the kitchen.

"Just a minute, young lady. You do not talk to me in that rash tone. Get your butt back out here," Grandmother demanded.

Annie's gaze bounced back and forth between them. She'd not seen her this angry since Annie and Mary drew lipstick patterns on one of the bedroom walls when they were kids. Or when they made mud pies and brought them inside. Or the time they captured some lizards and wanted to share them. She tried to hide the giggle that was building. This was beyond comical.

"Okay, folks. Let's all simmer down," Annie said, trying to play referee. "Grandmother, maybe you should be more specific in what you mean regarding this being their home and to make it comfortable."

"Well, I sure as heck didn't mean tear down wallpaper and give away chairs that cost me a fortune." She harrumphed.

"What is done is done, Sister," Patty said, finally finding her voice through the commotion.

Grandmother gave her a sideways glance. Clearing her throat, she began. "I would rather you see your time here at the house as more of a tenant and landlord relationship. You'd never just start pulling down wallpaper and painting walls without the landlord's permission."

"That's fine. Consider this our thirty-day notice, then." Mary crossed her arms at her chest while leering at Grandmother.

"Fine," Grandmother stated.

"Good," Mary said.

"Ladies," Patty interjected. "Is this what you want? Family to get all riled up over some paint and some ugly wallpaper."

"Ugly! Well, I never," Grandmother said, sticking her cane out at Patty and shaking it. "You always liked our décor here."

"It was always your home, Lilly. I just moved in. I'd never tell you how to furnish it, let alone decorate it. But I never loved those monkeys either." She nodded toward the wall.

"If I let you take the paper down and paint, what else are you going to do? You've already given away priceless furniture. I think maybe it is best if you and Danny move out, and Patty and I move back in."

Patty covered her mouth.

"That's not going to happen, Grandmother. You're too frail. I need to have you closer," Annie said.

"Frail? I'll have you know I am not frail. I may be getting up in years, but that's just a number. My mind is fully functional, and I am insulted you feel we can't live alone."

Annie tossed her hands up in the air and stomped her feet. "We are not having this discussion. You and Auntie are living in the cottage, and Mary and Danny are living here. Paint the walls striped. I don't care. Now, come on. I have a baby to attend to." Annie cradled Grandmother's elbow and led her out of the living room. Auntie followed behind. Grandmother kept stopping and looking back toward Mary and mouthing out demands and insults.

"You better not paint the walls striped. Leave the paper alone. I'm going to take an inventory of the furniture, young lady," she yelled out.

Annie ushered them outside and drew in a deep breath. She counted to ten before speaking. "Mary is your granddaughter. You just talked to her like she was some nobody standing on the corner. You've hurt her, I'm sure."

"Hurt her? She's hurt me." Grandmother pouted.

"I get it. This was your home for a good many years. And before that, it belonged to your parents. If you don't want her to make any changes, then she has to be able to move out. And if she moves out, what are we going to do with an empty house?"

"Take me home," Grandmother said, shaking loose Annie's grip.

THE RIDE HOME WAS EXCRUCIATING. Every time Annie thought about saying something, she quickly changed her mind. She had four people, if you counted Danny, all disappointed in the day's events. When she pulled up to the cottage she barely got the car in park before Grandmother hopped out. Frowning, Annie turned off the engine and stepped outside the car. "Are you going to pout like a baby or are we going to talk about this like adults?"

Grandmother and Auntie held hands as they ascended the steps. Once they got onto the porch, Patty fetched her key from her purse and unlocked the door. Helping her sister inside, she gave Annie a back-handed wave. "Bye, Annie," she said.

"Auntie Patty. Please talk to her."

"I hear you," Grandmother called out.

"Glad to hear that," Annie yelled back.

As Patty shut the door, she blew Annie a kiss. Shaking her head and grunting, she dropped into the driver's seat and drove around to the garages. Jack would be there, and he would solve all the problems of the world. Or at least with Grandmother and Mary.

She bolted through the back door and came into the house via the back porch. She traveled down the long hall. The noise coming from the other room had her picking up the pace. Widening her eyes, she watched as Ashton bounced on the couch cushions with his shoes on, dropping to his bottom and then jumping down, running to Isla and pulling her tail. Jack was in the kitchen with a towel draped over his shoulder, warming up a bottle and Carolina in his arms, screaming at the top of her lungs.

"Jack," she called.

He turned around, his face void of color except for two round red patches on his cheeks. Yellow gooey stuff soiled his shirt. He had something on his neck she didn't even want to know what it was, and when he came close enough to her, she wrinkled her nose.

"Let me have her." Annie held out her arms.

He gently rolled Carolina into her arms and took the towel away from his neck. "I'm exhausted."

She unbuttoned her blouse and sat while nursing Carolina. "Ashton Robert Powell. Stop jumping on the couch and stop teasing the dogs right this minute."

Ashton bounced one last time to his bottom and crossed his arms. "I'm hungry."

"Let me finish feeding your sister, and I'll fix you something."

"I don't know why he's hungry. He had a cookie, a bowl of chips, and a popsicle."

Annie tilted her head. "Sugar and carbs. Great. Okay, why don't you go take a shower. I'll put something together for us. I have a serious issue to discuss with you. I need your level head in this matter. I'm about to lose it with Grandmother."

AFTER ANNIE GOT the household settled, she made dinner. Nothing fancy, but edible. Grilled cheese sand-wiches and soup always worked in a pinch. She sliced an apple for them to share.

Now that Jack had showered, he smelled so much better. Annie wrapped her arms around him and kissed him. "I'm sorry you had such a hard time today. I didn't mean to be gone so long."

"No problem. I don't know how you do it."

She cocked her head.

"Take care of the kids, the house, and me."

"It's going to be a new thing now that we have two children. Some things aren't going to get done. Dinner might be late, the house might not be as clean, I might be tired—a lot, but we'll manage." She dropped a quick kiss on his nose.

"When do you think I should go back to work? The orders are piling up."

"Tomorrow," she said.

"Seriously?" She flashed a smile.

"Yes. But not before you solve this crisis."

"Let me tuck Ashton in, and I'll be right back. I do my best world problem solving with a glass of wine." He winked.

"I'll pour it and be waiting."

"So, let me get this straight. Mary wants to redo the old house, and Grandmother is not having it and has threatened to move back in. Where will Mary and Danny go? The cottage?"

"We didn't get that far. I can't let Grandmother and Auntie move back there. I'd be worried about them all the time."

"Well, to be fair, they did pretty good. Especially when we had caregivers Charles and Betsy there." Jack twirled his wine before sipping it.

"I know. All their friends are there, their social circles. But we're so far away if they need us."

"Let's see if we can find someone to move into the upstairs apartment," Jack said.

"Maybe. I don't know. I guess if I have to be completely honest, I'm not supervising them very well. Grandmother isn't eating properly; they sneak out and Uber into town. Living downtown couldn't be much worse, I suppose," she said, trailing off. "I'll discuss it with Grandmother in the morning."

"What you should do is give them an ultimatum. They only get to move back with full-time caregivers."

"Caregivers! They'd never go for that," Annie said.

"Call it whatever you want, but that's what they'll be," Jack said, nudging her shoulders gently.

CHAPTER 4

*A*nnie was happy that Grandmother and Auntie accepted her invitation to afternoon tea. She dusted the china teacups, tossed on a nice tablecloth, and put a vase of freshly cut roses on the table. Unfortunately, they would have store-bought cookies, but they loved shortbread, so they'd do in a pinch.

Carolina was sleeping soundly in the cradle Jack made. Ashton was sitting quietly coloring. Annie gave Jack time off and encouraged him to go outside and tinker. He didn't have to be told twice. He grabbed his hat, sunglasses, and a thermos and told her he'd be down at the dock, or in the garage.

Leaning in, he gave her a quick kiss. "Good luck."

"Thanks. They will be here any minute."

He held up his phone and flipped it around. "Call me if you need reinforcement."

The door pushed open and in stepped Grandmother and Auntie.

"Hello, Jack. Are you joining us today for tea?" Patty smiled.

"As much as I'd love to, I need to attend to a few things. You ladies have a great time." He bowed then exited swiftly.

"He's such a charming man. I only wished I'd have found him when I was searching for someone for you." Grandmother tiptoed over to the cradle and peered in. "So beautiful," she whispered.

Patty joined her. "A sleeping beauty," she said, nodding.

Grandmother gingerly stepped away from the cradle and, using her cane, moved to a chair.

Annie noticed the soft roundness of her shoulders, her less than perfectly straight posture. She sighed.

"China? Now, I'm impressed."

Annie pushed the platter with the shortbread cookies into the center of the table. "I'm sorry I didn't have time to bake. I hope these will suffice."

Grandmother's shoulders swayed.

"They're fine, Annie," Patty said, frowning toward Lilly.

"I suppose they are."

"Coming from the woman who eats boxed store-bought donuts," Annie sneered.

"Touché, Annie," Patty said.

"I learned from the best. Isn't that right, Grandmother?" Annie sat down.

Grandmother began to reach for the china-glazed teapot.

"Here, let me get that for you," Annie said, leaping up and leaning in.

"Annie. I'm quite capable of pouring my own tea."

"Of course, you are," she whispered, folding down to her chair like a shrinking violet.

"I've had time to think about the Mary situation," Grandmother said.

Annie paused, taking a bite of the cookie. "Oh?"

"Yes. We definitely want to move back into the house. But not before we can hire another person or couple to move upstairs. We discussed it, and you're right. We should have someone nearby. Mary can't be depended upon. She's such a scatter head."

Annie bit down on the cookie, crumbs scattering down her blouse. She then drew the cup to her mouth and washed it down.

"I suppose I'll reach out to the company who does this sort of thing and set up some interviews. I imagine you two will want to be in on those." She quirked her brow.

"Of course," Grandmother said, dipping the end of her shortbread into her tea and then quickly devouring it. "These are my favorite store-bought shortbread. They taste homemade." She smiled as she reached for another.

"Ahem. Grandmother. Sugar."

"I took my medication this morning. Can't I just have two?" she whined. "I'm eighty years old. I won't be around forever. Can't I just enjoy some pleasures in life?"

"Don't talk like that, Lilly," Patty said.

"It's true, Sister. Why be so restrictive with food and all of that when our time on earth is winding down."

"I just want you to be the healthiest you can be." Annie softened her stance.

"Let Mary know of our decision, won't you?" Grandmother said, sliding her chair back.

"I will. And I'll get right on it regarding caregivers."

"Caregivers!" Grandmother shouted, nearly waking up Carolina.

"Well, not caregivers exactly," Annie said, trying to take it back. "Live-in help?" she said, scrambling for words.

"You can call it what you want, but Patty and I see it as more of a joint arrangement. There will be times when we need them, but hopefully, it will be few and far between. Knowing someone is near is all we want." She stood.

"Grandmother, I'm feeling guilty because I can't be the one for you. I was so hoping the cottage would work out for you both. I know you feel isolated, but we are trying to include you in our lives, and we do understand your need for independence." Annie lowered her gaze to the table.

"I love the cottage," Patty said. "I love being out in the country and near the water. It's lovely."

"You do?" Annie said.

Patty nodded. "The big house in Charleston is drafty. And it does flood downtown, making it a mess to get around. And Mary is right. The wallpaper is creepy."

Grandmother gasped. "Patty Bolander!"

"It's true, Lilly. I feel quite content here. I don't want to move again."

"But when we discussed it last night—"

"You did all the talking. I just listened."

Grandmother hung her head and tapped her cane twice. "I suppose this new revelation changes things."

Annie's gaze flipped from Patty to Lilly.

"We'll put the property up for sale," Grandmother said.

"I'm not suggesting that, Grandmother."

"I know. But it's the only thing left to do. It's starting

to deteriorate. We don't have the time or the energy to take that on. Mary was just trying to do us a favor. It's not fair to straddle her with such an obligation."

Annie widened her eyes. "Take some time to think it over. We don't have to rush."

"Yes, Lilly. Sleep on it." Patty touched her sister's arm.

"I'll ask Mary to stay on until you've made a decision. We wouldn't want the house with all of your stuff sitting unoccupied," Annie said.

Grandmother shook her head. "So much to do. That house holds a lot of memories and things. The cottage will not hold another item."

"But you can take all the memories with you," Annie said. "The other stuff. It's just stuff." She slipped her arm around Grandmother's shoulders. "You have pictures to look at too. And if not, we'll make sure we take them so you'll have them to look back on."

Grandmother looked up. A tear bobbled on her lower lid. "Thank you, Annie. You've been wonderful. Both you and Jack have done so much for Lilly and me."

"Mary's tried too. She's young. She's doing the best she knows how," Patty said to her sister.

"I suppose," Grandmother grunted.

"She loves you both," Annie said, agreeing with Patty's statement.

"It's five o'clock somewhere, right?" Grandmother rested her hand on the doorknob.

Annie giggled. "Yes, Grandmother. But please—"

Grandmother held up a finger to shush her.

"Don't drink and drive," Annie said.

"Now, that's better," Grandmother said, blowing her a kiss.

Annie stood in amazement as she watched her two favorite old people in the world hobble out of her house and down the stairs. "Never underestimate a McPherson," Annie said just above a whisper.

"Mommy," Ashton called out.

He'd been so quiet coloring Annie almost forgot he was in the room.

"Yes?"

"Look at my picture."

Annie wandered over to the couch and sat, picking up the coloring book. "This is so nice, Ashton. You're doing so well with staying in the lines."

"That's Lady Powell," he said, using a blue crayon as a pointer.

"And you colored it very nicely. Daddy will like that."

She rolled her wrist to take a look at the time. Carolina would be waking up soon. Two hours went by so fast.

After Annie fed Carolina and started dinner, Jack came waltzing back inside. Whistling a catchy tune and grinning ear to ear, he dropped a quick kiss on Annie's forehead. Lifting the lid to the pot on the stove, he took a long sniff. "Yum. Seafood gumbo."

"I had fresh shrimp to use up," Annie said, giving the soup a stir.

"How'd things go with the young-at-heart ladies next door?" Jack sniggered.

"Actually, you'll be very pleased. Pour yourself a glass of wine and take a seat. It's pretty interesting."

"Care to join me?"

"Just a smidgeon," Annie said.

Jack set the table and poured their wine. He washed Ashton's hands and set him on the booster seat in the chair. He'd recently announced that highchairs were for babies, and Carolina could have his.

Annie spooned out pieces of shrimp and potatoes for Ashton, then ladled soup into bowls for Jack and herself. And with baby Carolina cradled in her arm, Annie quickly filled Jack in while slurping her soup.

"Seriously? They came to the conclusion on their own it was better for them to stay in the cottage? I wished I had been a fly on the wall." Jack picked up his wineglass and swirled the contents.

"I think Auntie was the defining moment. She flat out told Grandmother she liked it here. Didn't want to move."

"Do you think they'll sell the place?" Jack forked a large shrimp.

"I think so. But it won't happen overnight. We have a lot of stuff to go through. That house holds so many memories, both physical and mental."

"I'm happy to help. I know Danny and my brother-in-law, Richard will, and even my mom and dad. It will be a concerted effort." Jack reached across the table and held his hand open. Annie slid her hand into his. "We're in this together for better or worse, remember?" He winked.

"I love you, Jack. It's going to be pretty dramatic. I know for sure I will need them to make the first move in all of this. It has to be on their terms. Whatever they say, we do." She tipped her chin.

CHAPTER 5

*I*t was two months to the day when they had tea, and Grandmother and Auntie decided to stay on at the cottage. Two months and no more had been said. Mary was hounding Annie constantly, wanting to know when she and Danny could move out. Annie didn't have an answer because nothing was ever planned. Caught up in motherhood, she let it sit on the back burner. But now it was nearing fall time, and a great time for cleaning out closets and sprucing up places, and Annie made the decision to approach them about things before Mary did. And everyone knew Mary had no time for fluffing feathers. Her approach would be anything but soft.

The temperatures had dropped, and so had the leaves of the many trees on the property. The vivid green and glossy leaves of the stately magnolia added a splash of color among the yellow and red leaves of the various oaks and native varieties. Annie drew her sweater close and pulled in a deep breath of the clean, refreshing air. "Here goes nothing," she said, stepping down from the porch.

Rapping on the door, she waited for them to respond.

"Hello," Annie said, closing the door behind her.

"Is it that time?" Patty asked, grabbing her shawl that had been draped over a chair.

"Where's Grandmother?"

"In the little girl's room," Auntie said, wrapping the end of her shawl up over her shoulder.

"Listen, Auntie Patty. Have you and Grandmother discussed anymore about the Charleston house?"

Patty shook her head. "I've tried to approach the subject a few times. She was so for it before. I don't know what's happened."

"Is she still considering moving back into it?"

"No, I don't think so. She may not want to admit it, but she knows we're better off here. And now that Jack's dad is coming once a week and taking us into town, it's been nice."

"Yes, I think it's very sweet Robert is doing that."

Just then, they turned their attention to the clipping noise of Grandmother's cane.

"Hope you have a good appetite. I made lasagna," Annie said.

"As long as you have a nice red to go with it." Patty smirked.

"Yes, Auntie. I always have a nice bottle of red in the rack."

She tried not to mother them too much, but she stood by as they walked over to the main house. Annie watched carefully, and Grandmother appeared to be pretty stable on her feet. As Annie stared at her shoes, her jaw dropped. Grandmother had on orthopedic shoes. For as long as she could remember, Grandmother and Auntie wore the latest designs and matching shoes to go with them. They'd never be caught in orthopedic anything. But times were changing, and no matter how hardheaded Grandmother was, she also knew when she'd lost the battle.

She couldn't help herself and offered a hand to the ladies as they ascended the stairs. Surprisingly, neither of them opposed her gesture.

"Something smells wonderful," Patty said, making her way to the couch to join Ashton. She held out her arms, and he climbed onto her lap.

"Hello, Jack," Grandmother said, slipping into a chair at the dining table.

"Good evening, ladies," he said.

Patty smiled and then went back to talking to Ashton.

"Fall is in the air, isn't it?" he said as he popped the cork on the wine.

"Perfect time to clean out garages and closets," Annie said, taking the cue.

"And painting. Well, any type of repair or maintenance to property. I've got a few things to do here," Jack said.

Annie's gazed bobbled from Grandmother to Auntie and back to Jack. Had he said too much? Nothing got by these two.

"What sort of things do you have to do here?" Grandmother said.

"The front porch needs a coat of paint, for one," Jack said.

Annie listened as this conversation went on and on. Finally, convinced that either they were not getting the big picture, or they were trying to string poor Jack along, Annie put a stop to it.

"Have you spoken to Mary, Grandmother?" Annie asked as she took the casserole dish from the oven and set it on a trivet to cool.

"No."

"Oh," Annie said, leaning her back up against the counter. "Is something wrong?"

"No. Why would you think that?"

"I don't know. Maybe because it's been a while, and you haven't reached out to her about the house."

"The house?" She cocked her head. "What is it that I need to discuss with my flighty granddaughter regarding my property? Please enlighten me."

Jack poured more wine, lifting his glass and drinking. Annie kept her gaze on him before turning her attention to Lilly. "You don't have to discuss any financial things with her, but you did say she could move out. She's waiting for that day."

"Ahh," Grandmother said. "She can move out whenever she wants. We're not stopping her."

"Grandmother Lilly. Stop playing games. You said you would consider selling the property. You can't just drop it on us one day. It takes planning. The house needs some repairs, we have stuff to go through, and it will take weeks if not months to do all of that. The weather is nice now, and we can get a lot accomplished."

"It's overwhelming to think about it all," Grandmother said, lowering her gaze.

"I know it is. But we're here to help," Annie said, moving to Grandmother's side.

Finally speaking up, Patty offered some advice. "We'll start with the closets. Then we'll move to the furniture."

"We?" Grandmother sneered.

"Yes, we. It'll be fun. Annie, Mary, you and me. We'll get out the boxes of pictures and memorabilia and go through them. It will help with the process. The girls might want some of it too."

"Give me the phone," Grandmother demanded.

Annie moved quickly and obeyed, handing her the cell phone.

She moved the phone in and out as she adjusted her sights. "Oh, just call her," she said, handing Annie the phone.

"It's ringing," she said as she handed it back to Grandmother.

While Annie served up the lasagna, they listened as Grandmother spoke to Mary. It was short and sweet, but Grandmother got her point across. She gave Mary permission to start looking for places to live, and also about the idea of going through the boxes.

"Satisfied?" Grandmother said, tossing the phone down. "It's all settled. Danny and Mary will start looking for a new place, and we'll go through the decades of memories and get it ready to sell."

"Grandmother. It's not me who you have to satisfy."

"Lilly. It's time," Patty said.

"All right. I reserve the right to wait on my satisfaction until I hear the amount we'll receive for such a historical property."

"I'm sure you'll fetch a very fair price. It's a beautiful house, Lilly," Jack said.

"I guess we might as well enjoy you all appreciating your inheritance while we're still around to see it," Lilly said.

"It's not about inheriting money, Grandmother. It's about letting you have a voice in how things are done before you're gone. It has to give you some comfort to know that your wishes will be honored because you're around to see it done."

"My real wishes were to keep the house in the family. But that's not to be." A tear bobbled on her lower lid.

"I'm sorry it didn't work out that way. Jack and I have our place here on the island. We can't move into Charleston," Annie said.

"It would be closer to the bakery," Lilly said.

"Yes, but I'm not even going there very often. In fact, I've been considering letting someone take it over."

Patty gasped. Grandmother snarled.

"Jack's wood business has taken off. He can't even keep up with the orders. He needs help."

"How are you going to help?" Patty asked.

"Bookkeeping, taking orders, marketing, that sort of thing."

"That would be a great help to him, I'm sure," Patty said.

"Well, isn't this just dandy. Everyone's life is being uprooted. We're selling our family home and destroying the last historical artifact we have of the McPherson name; Annie is going to hand over her business she started from the ground up, and we'll all just be happy as clams." Grandmother snorted.

Annie's gaze wandered to Jack. Nodding once toward the wine, he picked up the bottle and topped everyone's glass off.

CHAPTER 6

*A*nnie should have known that nothing happened quickly concerning Grandmother, but taking another thirty days before she'd agree to a trip over to the house was a tad much. But being sensitive to the matter, Annie and Mary both agreed that giving her the time she needed was better in the long run. So, when Lilly broached the subject while rocking on the back porch, watching long-neck cranes searching for food, Annie almost fell out of the chair.

"Okay," Annie said

"I know you and Mary must be chomping at the bit." Lilly rolled her neck toward Annie and smirked.

"Now, Grandmother. That's not fair. We're both trying to be sensitive regarding this. We're just waiting for you to tell us when."

"Mary never calls to see how we are doing," she blurted.

Annie sighed. "I don't know what to say. She's a newlywed."

Lilly narrowed her brows. "What's that supposed to mean? That they can't come up for a breath from rolling in the hay to call and see how Patty and I are doing?"

Annie's mouth dropped open. "No, she does ask. She asks me."

Lilly waved off Annie's excuses with a brush of her hand. "Anyway, let's get it set up for this weekend. I'd rather it be just us. No Danny."

"I'll tell her."

ANSWERING the door in a silk poncho in a paisley design of green and orange on a cream background, Mary ushered them inside. She pecked Grandmother's cheek, then turning to the other, gave her another quick kiss. She repeated the same with Auntie Patty.

"Those colors are gorgeous with your hair color, Mary," Patty said.

"Why, thank you, Auntie." Mary glowed.

"I have tea and biscuits in the living room. Please, come in."

Grandmother and Auntie made their way into the living room where boxes and containers were stacked on either side of the room. Annie's gaze drifted around the room.

"I see you've been busy," Annie said.

"Yes, I had Danny go up in the attic and bring down boxes. Thought we could start there."

Grandmother and Auntie sat on the couch and clasped their hands in their laps.

"I know it seems overwhelming, but we'll take all the time we need," Annie said, reassuring them this did not have to be completed today.

"Let's start by opening one of the boxes, sip some tea, eat some cookies, and just search through the contents." Mary tugged one of the boxes closer to them and opened the flaps.

Annie poured the tea, sitting opposite of Grandmother and Auntie in a chair Mary had borrowed from the dining room.

Mary pulled out a stack of papers and tossed them on the corner of the coffee table. Lilly leaned forward and flipped through them. "These have no value. We can toss these."

"Are you sure?" Annie asked.

Grandmother tipped her forehead.

Mary leaped from her chair and hurried to the

kitchen. Upon her return, she held a large black plastic bag. She reached for the bundle of papers and threw them inside.

They went through one box in about fifteen minutes. This was going better than Annie or Mary could have hoped for. Breaking down the empty box, Mary set it up against the wall and lugged another toward them. She peeked inside. "Pictures," she said, lifting out several photo books, loose pictures, and a few boxes of slides.

Each woman took a photo book and began to scan through pages.

"Oh, I remember this picture." Annie turned the book around and shared the image.

"Your first day of seventh grade," Auntie said.

"You remember it was my first day of seventh grade?" Annie shrugged.

Void of happiness, eyes wet and dull, Patty said, "I do. It was a very emotional time for you. For both of you girls."

Annie dropped her gaze back to the photo. The memories came rushing in. Her mother had recently passed away after a long and courageous battle. Annie felt alone and lost. Her father and grandmother, along with Auntie, tried to carry on with as much normalcy as they could. Mary was just five years old. Their dad, a military man, standing tall and brave, never shed a tear in front of them. Years later, he'd tell her he would bawl like a baby behind closed doors. Thank God for Grandmother Lilly and Auntie Patty.

"It's coming back to me. I remember the outfit now. I didn't want to wear it, but you insisted that Mom had picked it out for me. She'd hoped to see me in it, but that wasn't to be." Annie placed the picture in a pile, turning her attention to the box.

"Your father was so strong," Grandmother said. "My heart broke for him."

"I remember that day too. It was my first day in kindergarten," Mary said.

All eyes turned to her.

"I didn't want to go to school. Dad told me that Mom would be watching over me that day, and if I didn't go, she'd be all alone there." A small giggle escaped her mouth. "So, I went because, of course, I didn't want to disappoint her."

"Your mother was a very courageous woman. She fought the tough battle with that C-word," Patty said. "Is there any alcohol here? I think I need a drink."

"Wine. Would that work?" Mary soared out of the chair.

"Let me help you," Annie said.

Mary popped the cork on a merlot. "I don't want today to be a sad, Debbie Downer sort of day." She took a wineglass out of Annie's hand and began to fill it.

"I think it's good to go down memory lane. We don't talk about Mom and Dad enough," Annie said, handing her the next glass.

"For the longest time, I couldn't. I had so many emotions and feelings about it all. One minute we had her, and the next we didn't." Mary took two of the glasses and held them by the stems.

Annie reached for the remaining two wineglasses. "I know, Mary. And I know Grandmother, Auntie, and Dad sheltered us from the real pain. She was dying before our eyes, yet, as children we probably didn't know the extent of it. But I bet he sure did."

"This house holds a lot of memories because after Dad was killed, we moved in here. Our entire life was disrupted."

"We got hit with a double whammy, didn't we?" Mary took the lead and moved out of the kitchen toward the living room.

"Yes, but I'm so thankful we had them," she said, motioning toward the two women looking at pictures and other memorabilia.

"I'm thankful I have you," Annie said, fighting back tears.

"Ahh. That's sweet. I guess I'm thankful for you too.

Although I'd wish you weren't quite so bossy." She winked.

Both women took a deep breath and then, with heads held high, entered the room.

"Here we go," Mary said, handing Grandmother a glass of wine.

Patty gripped her glass with two hands and took an immediate sip.

"Look at these oldies but goodies," Lilly said.

Over the course of the next four hours, the women went through two bottles of wine while going through four boxes. They made piles of pictures for Mary and Annie to scan, a pile of stuff to toss, and a pile of letters that also brought back a lot of memories.

"To my Dearest Lilly. I miss you more each day. My days are kept busy, but my nights are lonely, and I long for the day I'm home and in your arms."

"Ahh. That's so sweet, Grandmother," Mary said.

"Yes, that's so long ago, though. I don't need to keep love letters from Chester."

"Oh look. A picture of Grandfather," Annie said, holding up a picture of a dashing man in a uniform.

"Now that I will keep," Grandmother said, snatching the picture out of Annie's hand.

The women broke out in laughter.

"Are you sure you can preserve these by scanning them?" Lilly asked.

"Yes. I'll take them to Costco. They do a fabulous job. They'll put them on a disc. Then we'll have them to pass down to Ashton and Carolina."

"And any grandchildren from Mary and Danny," Patty said.

"Yes. Of course." Annie looked at her watch. "It's getting late. I need to get back to Magnolia and save Jack from the children."

"We can't just leave everything in disarray." Lilly looked around at the piles of pictures and boxes stacked along the wall.

"It's okay, Grandmother," Mary said. "We should set up another time to finish going through the boxes."

They all agreed they'd meet again the following day, but after Annie got them home, and she and Jack were catching up, the phone rang, and in a matter of five seconds, everyone was back on the hamster wheel.

CHAPTER 7

With the phone plastered against her head, her pulse thumping loudly inside her ear, she listened to Mary. Pausing a moment, she gathered her thoughts.

"Mary, are you sure this is what you want, and not the wine talking?"

"The wine may have amplified my feelings, but it's the right thing to do. The house means so much to Grandmother. Her entire life was spent here. Some of our saddest times were spent here, and some of our happiest times were here."

"What about the drafty windows, and the outdated furnishings?"

"I can wait on all of that. Grandmother won't be here

forever. I can live with it the way it is. It brings her joy, and at her age, what else can she ask for?"

A small tear dribbled down Annie's cheek. Mary sounded so grown up. And she was so caring. It made her heart swell with love.

"Mary, that is so sweet of you. But if you and Danny decide to stay there, we can't have a bunch of back and forth on this. It's not fair to them. If you stay on, you stay on until…until I say you can move on." She gulped, waiting for Mary to become outraged at her stance.

But Mary didn't argue one bit. In fact, she was more than agreeable, surprising Annie once again with her new and improved little sister attitude.

"I agree. I promise to stay until you say I can move. I won't make any drastic changes. I also contacted the charity I gave the chairs to after you all left. They still had them. I explained everything, and they said if we pick them up, we can have them back. Danny and I are going tomorrow."

Annie recalled how upset Grandmother was over the chintz-covered chairs. "That's great news. I wish we had extra wallpaper."

"I think I can salvage that too. There might just be a small sliver of damaged paper. I think I can cover it up with paint. Feather it in somehow. I'll put a tall houseplant up against it, or maybe a piece of furniture. I'm good at hiding flaws. It will be all right."

"Mary Powell. I'm so proud of you at this moment. I've always admired your spunk and tenacity, but sometimes you can be a bit selfish. But not today. You've come out in true McPherson fashion. I think Grandmother would love to hear about your decision in person. You and Danny come over tomorrow for Sunday dinner. It's supposed to be a beautiful evening. We'll toss a few logs on the outdoor firepit. It'll be fun."

"I love you, Sis," Mary said.

"I love you too," Annie said, wiping another stray tear as it slid down her face.

GRANDMOTHER AND AUNTIE showed up promptly at six. As long as Annie could remember, those two ladies were never late for anything, especially an invitation to dinner. Dressed in dark jeans, plaid flannel shirt, and suede boots with a small heel, Patty sported the cutest red beret while Grandmother wore a more traditional tam in plaid. Drawing off their woolen capes from their shoulders, Jack quickly hung them up on the coat rack near the door.

Grandmother casually entered the kitchen and lifted the cover off the pot on the stove and peered in.

"Beef stew?" She wrinkled her nose before lowering the lid.

"Yes. I hope that's all right?" Annie said.

"It sounds delicious to me, Annie," Patty said, coming into the kitchen.

Lilly raised her brow. "I didn't say it didn't."

"I wasn't sure when you wrinkled your nose." Annie flashed a half-cocked smile.

"I don't know why she did that. She loves beef stew," Patty interjected.

"I never said I didn't." Lilly crossed over to Patty and stood nose to nose with her.

Annie whirled around, placing her hands on their shoulders. "Ladies. Let's take a seat and have a glass of iced tea while we wait for Mary and Danny."

"Iced tea. I need something stronger than that. My arthritis is flaring up again. It must have been from searching through all those boxes," Grandmother said.

Annie let out a long breath while she led them to the table. Looking over her shoulder at Jack, she shrugged. He read her mind, rushing toward the counter where the bottle sat.

Jack filled the ladies' glasses and made sure he handed Annie hers first. While she sipped, she finished dinner, putting the salad mix in a large bowl, and popping the biscuits into the oven.

A whoosh of air came inside as Mary and Danny came laughing in.

"The wind has picked up. I'm not sure if we'll be able to have the fire tonight," Mary said, walking over to Grandmother and kissing her on the cheek, then turning to Auntie and planting a big kiss on her mouth. Patty giggled. "Your lips are cold," she said.

"It's a little chilly outside, Auntie Patty," Mary said, shivering.

"Well, we'll see how it is after dinner. Help me dish up the stew," Annie said.

Annie listened as Jack, Danny, Grandmother, and Auntie talked about various topics. Those two were well versed in countless topics, keeping up to date with politics, weather, and the stock market. In between their discussion, Ashton screamed for attention. Carolina was fast asleep in her cradle, and Annie was finding she was getting used to Ashton's loudness, sleeping through most of it.

The lively conversation continued around the dinner table, when Mary suddenly blurted out her news, making Grandmother drop her spoon into her stew, splattering brown gravy everywhere.

"You're going to do what?" Grandmother squinted her eyes.

"We've decided to stay in the house. It'll be fine. I

shouldn't have been such a whiney baby about the wallpaper and all. It's actually growing on me." She shrugged.

"Let me get this straight. You've put me through hell for the past few weeks, giving me total anxiety of what to do regarding my things and property, and now, you suddenly have an epiphany moment where it might not be in the best interest of the family to move out?"

Annie switched her gaze back and forth without moving her head. Should she soften the blow, intervene on Mary's behalf? She sank into her chair and watched as it unfolded.

"I thought you'd be pleased," Mary said, barely above a whisper.

"Well, I'm not." Grandmother harrumphed.

"Grandmother, if I may. I think what Mary is trying to say, she has had time to think about it. All of what it entails, and she's willing to stay on. I thought you'd find it comforting," Annie said, tipping her head as she smiled at Auntie Patty.

"I would have found it comforting had she not thrown a total hissy fit from the beginning. How do we know she won't change her mind again?" Lilly spat she was so angry.

Danny cleared his throat, his mouth gathering as he formed sounds.

Annie's heart began to beat hard, and knowing what was about to happen, she tried to head it off, but it was too late. She sighed.

"Lilly. Please don't be so hard on Mary. She was torn between wanting her own place and preserving the old homestead. It doesn't matter when her realization came, does it?" Danny said.

Grandmother cut her eyes to Danny, her jaw dropping as she stared at him.

Jack slid out his chair and announced he was getting more wine. "Danny, can you help me, please."

Annie knew exactly what Jack was doing. Giving her more time to smooth things over.

"Auntie Patty, how do you feel about all of this? You're being rather quiet," Annie said.

Patty tilted her head and let out a deep breath. "Actually, I don't know why your grandmother is making such a fuss over this. This is what she wanted. Mary is staying on in the house. We're staying put at the cottage. All is well that ends well." She turned her head toward Lilly and raised her brows. "Don't you think, Sister?"

Lilly pointed her spoon at Mary. "Mary McPherson Powell. Let this be a warning. Don't come to me next week or next month and tell us you've changed your mind. My emotions cannot handle that."

"I promise. I wanted to let you know that we got your

chairs back, and Danny and I've repaired the wallpaper. There's just a tiny spot that we weren't able to salvage. I moved the potted palm over to cover it."

"That palm will not survive there. It likes to be over by the window," Lilly spouted.

"Grandmother. Mary is trying. Please meet her half-way," Annie said.

Jack and Danny came back to the table and sat.

"I'm tired of this conversation. Let's move on. I can feel my blood pressure rising."

"I do think it's a good idea we continue to go through boxes and things," Mary said.

Grandmother's glare sparked a quick response from Mary.

"At your leisure, of course," Mary added.

After dinner, Annie loaded the sink with the dishes and ushered everyone outside, after Danny and Jack had determined the wind had died down, and it would be perfect for a fire.

Bundling up the women with their cloaks, Annie also pulled out a few lap blankets to take outside.

"I'll be out soon. I need to feed and change Carolina. Can you handle them and Ashton?" Annie nodded toward Grandmother and Auntie.

"Of course. Ashton, take my hand," Mary

commanded. Grandmother, place your arm through Patty's, and Auntie, you hold my other hand."

Annie helped them out and down the stairs then went back inside to attend to Carolina.

WHEN ANNIE finally made it outside with Carolina, the fire was roaring, and flames about two feet high danced in the night air. Bundled up under their blankets, Grandmother and Patty shared a comfortable wooden bench with a back that Jack had made, and cushions that Jack's mother made especially for it. Mary sat in one of the Adirondack chairs with Ashton on her lap. Danny and Jack sat near each other, poking the fire, laughing and talking.

Annie sat in the other Adirondack chair, making sure Carolina was covered head to toe. Snuggling her tightly toward her chest, she watched the flames flicker in the dark.

"What a gorgeous evening," Patty said.

"Kiawah in the late fall. It doesn't get much better than this," Jack said, looking up.

"I love this time of year. Less heat and humidity," Mary said.

"The older I get, the less I like the humidity," Annie said, agreeing with Mary.

"Oh, please. You crybabies. Back in the day, we didn't even have air conditioning. August was so hot and humid, and opening the windows did very little to help us escape the horrific heat. So instead of complaining, we used to strip down to our undies and sleep out on the porch under the veranda. We'd splash cool water on us and fan our faces with homemade fans. When we were able to get air conditioning we had it installed, but I sort of miss the good old days of sitting out on the porch during the night and watching fireflies, and taking in the sweet aroma of mock orange and tea olive plants in the garden."

"I have to say, Lilly, I agree. Those were simpler days, were they not?" Patty shifted her weight on the bench.

Annie could see their expressions as the glow of the fire lit up their faces. They were happy, and Annie had a difficult time hiding her emotions.

"I know we have our disagreements. What family doesn't? But I want everyone around this firepit to know, I love you. I can't imagine my life without you, and I hope we have many more nights sitting around, laughing and reminiscing about the good old days," Annie said.

"Mommy. Do I have old days?" Ashton said.

Everyone's jovial outbursts made Carolina jerk in Annie's arms, her little hands flailing out of the blanket, followed by a small whimper. Annie immediately began rocking her. Everyone stopped making a single sound, and all eyes were on Carolina. The fire snapped, crackled, and popped. Ashton shushed the fire. Grandmother smirked, Patty sniggered, and Annie beamed with happiness as she studied her somewhat opinionated, sometimes cranky, but in the end, always supportive family.

When everyone agreed they'd had enough bonding, Grandmother and Auntie stood and announced they were ready to retire to the cottage.

Jack doused the flames with a little water and poked the logs around. Mary helped Grandmother and Auntie into the cottage, leaving Annie and Danny and the children behind to clean up.

"It's past these kiddo's bedtime," Annie said, taking Ashton by the hand as she held Carolina tightly to her body.

"I know I married into the family, but Mary is my wife," Danny said.

Annie stared at him. "What do you mean, Danny?"

"I just feel that sometimes y'all gang up on her. That's why I spoke out about the housing arrangement," he said.

"We don't gang up on Mary," Annie said, perturbed. "Most of the time, she asks for it."

"So, do you or don't you gang up on her?" Danny stepped closer toward her.

Jack dropped the poker stick and moved in between them. "Danny. Back off. This is my wife you're talking to."

Annie stepped out and around the men and headed toward the house. She was in no mood to defend her sister, especially to Jack's cousin. As she made her way toward the steps of Sweet Magnolia, the cottage door flew open and out danced a laughing Mary.

"Hey, Sis. Do you need any help putting the children down?"

"No, but your husband may need some help." She motioned her head toward the men.

They both could hear their voices elevating in the darkness. "What happened?" Mary asked.

"He felt he needed to come to the rescue of your honor. He got a bit accusatory in his tone, so Jack is giving him a dose of it back, I'm afraid."

"Is this over the house?" Mary asked

"I think so. I don't know. He thinks we gang up on you."

"You do."

"Mary McPherson, err, Powell. We do not."

"Please. I can never do anything right. I'm the

younger sister, the flighty one. Isn't that what you all call me?"

Annie's gaze flitted to the guys then back to her sister. "Mary. Don't. I'm tired, the children are tired, and it's cold outside. Take your husband home and get some sleep. I think the wine is talking for the both of you tonight."

Annie moved a few more steps toward the house.

"I've never been good enough for any of you. I don't care how you see me, what you think of me, or any of that. I made a promise to Grandmother and Auntie about staying in the house, and I will. Danny and I have some plans of our own. You just wait and see."

Annie whirled around, dragging Ashton while holding his hand.

"Don't threaten me, Mary. It won't work. Now go home. Tomorrow I'll be waiting for my apology. Jack! Time to come in. Danny and Mary are leaving." Annie's voice carried deep into the woods.

"Danny, come on," Mary echoed. "I'm ready to get the heck off this island." Mary crossed her arms and glared.

"Auntie Mary, are you mad at Mommy?" Ashton said.

Mary dropped down to his eye level. "No, honey.

We're just a bit tired and cold is all. Sweet dreams." She kissed him on his cheek.

Annie twisted her mouth tightly and squinted at Mary. "Good night, Mary."

"Good night, Sis."

Jack rushed up beside Annie and pulled Ashton up and over his shoulders. Annie could hear Danny whispering as they veered another direction to where their car was parked.

"I'll get this all ironed out tomorrow. I'll have a little come to Jesus with old Danny Boy," Jack said, opening the screen door.

"I think they just had a bit too much wine to drink and felt froggy. Mary has always felt like we were challenging her on things. She has a vivid imagination."

"I'm just glad Lilly and Patty weren't around to hear all of it."

Danny dropped the gear down low on his car and while kicking up sand and rocks, sped down the road, past Scott and Vicky's house. She'd have to apologize for the ruckus to Vicky tomorrow.

CHAPTER 8

*T*he temperatures dipped low overnight, and when they awoke, frost glistened off the glossy magnolia tree leaves and on patches of grass underneath the treas. The gloomy sky just added to her miserable mood. Bundling up both children in their winter gear, Annie headed over to the Collins' house. She needed a friendly face and an ear to bend.

Vicky helped by hanging up jackets and scarves then led them to the living room where a roaring fire danced inside the fireplace. Jasmine was sitting in the middle of the floor, playing with dolls.

"Coffee, tea?" Vicky asked.

"Coffee sounds divine," Annie said. "Why don't you go play with Jasmine?" She lifted a brow to Ashton.

He moved slowly over to the area where dolls were stacked, mostly with their hair messed up, and their clothes on backward.

Vicky soon brought in the beverages and sat the cups on the coffee table. "It's downright cold." She hugged her arms.

"I know. We sat outside last night and had a bonfire. The wind had died down, and it didn't seem so cold. But this morning…a whole other story." She leaned forward and picked up a cup.

"I was just finishing up cleaning the kitchen when I heard Danny race out of here. What was his issue?" Vicky sipped her coffee.

"We had words. I'm apologizing for his behavior. We're so sorry he tore out of here. That was immature of him."

"At first, I wondered if something had happened to Lilly or Patty. I waited a little bit before retiring to bed. Figured you'd let me know."

"No, they're fine." Annie shook her head. "You know Mary. Drama queen through and through. And now she's training Danny to be a drama king." She laughed.

"Are they still moving out of the Charleston home?"

"No. That's all changed now. They're staying put. It's like being on a Ferris wheel with those two. Well, mainly Mary. Danny is just going along for the ride."

"Are Lilly and Patty all right with the new arrangements?"

"Yes, I believe so. Actually, relieved is a better word. It was overwhelming for them to even think about moving back in, and selling, well that was the worst of it." Annie studied Ashton and Jasmine while they played dolls. He was being so kind.

"I'm glad it worked out. I think they're better off at the cottage where you can keep an eye on them."

"Yes, I do too. So, tell me, when are you two headed to Korea?" Annie flashed a warm smile.

"Next week. We're super excited. We have all our passports ready, all the documentation ready, and of course, the funds are being held in a trust until we get our sweet boy." Vicky's lids grew red, and tears welled up at the bottom.

"I can't wait to meet him. I mean, *we* can't wait," Annie said, looking over at Carolina in her car seat, sleeping soundly.

"Would you all keep an eye on the place while we're gone? I don't expect anything to happen, with you being so close by, and of course, we'll have the alarm on as well." Vicky nodded toward the children. "Ashton is such a nice boy. I'm so happy Jasmine has him as a friend."

"I love that our children are growing up together. Soon we'll have little—" Her jaw dropped. "What did you decide to name him?" Annie asked, realizing she didn't know what their son's name was.

"We thought about it long and hard. Think we're going to stick with J's and call him Jackson. Do you think that will be too weird with you all living nearby?"

"Only if you decide to call him Jack for short. Then we might." Annie covered her mouth to squelch her hearty laugh.

"Nope, it will always be Jackson. Jackson Scott. Has a great ring, don't you think?"

"It does. I'm so happy for you both."

The two women held their cups to their lips and took a sip, all the while watching the children play.

"Have you given any more thought about an early retirement from the bakery business?" Vicky asked.

"I think about it all the time. I don't want to make any rash decisions regarding it. I'd thought maybe Mary would like to dive in and help me run it, but I'm not sure I can count on her."

"You have a great team in place now. What's the guy's name..."

"Peter. Yes, he's taken on so much since I left. I could see him being the owner. But with it being a woman-operated business for so long, I was just hoping to hand over the reins to another woman entrepreneur."

"True, but then where does that leave poor Peter?" With a puzzling look painted on her face, Vicky shrugged.

Tipping her chin, a small moan escaped Annie's mouth. "True," she whispered.

CHAPTER 9

*S*tanding at the sink, Annie stared out the window in a daze as she swished the dishrag around. Deeply enthralled in watching the trees sway and a few birds hopping around from limb to limb, she didn't even hear Jack come in. Flinching as he wrapped his arms around her waist, Annie let out a small explicative at the same time she whirled around in his arms.

"Hi, I didn't mean to startle you." He leaned in and kissed her.

"I was a million miles away."

"I can see that. What's on your mind?" He moved away from her and opened the cabinet nearby, retrieving a glass.

"Oh, this and that." She turned and finished what she

was doing at the sink. "We're having grilled cheese and tomato soup for dinner. Hope that's okay."

"That's perfect," he said.

"Carolina is taking a nap; Ashton is over at the cottage. He's been over there for twenty minutes, and I haven't received any sort of SOS from them." She laughed.

"I better go save the day," he said, throwing back the glass of water he'd just poured.

"They're coming for dinner. At least that's what they said. I told them all we were having was grilled cheese and soup. They said it sounded lovely to them." Annie shrugged.

Jack was almost to the front door. "It's probably more about just hanging out with us. It's not about the food." He turned the knob and opened the door. "I'll be back in a jiffy."

Closing the door behind him, Jack paused a moment, taking in the beautiful scenery of Sweet Magnolia. He had to pinch himself often, reminding himself this was theirs. His and Annie's and their sweet children. A place for them to grow old and a place for the kids to grow up.

Sighing, he descended the few stairs and jogged over to the cottage. He rapped twice before opening the door.

"Hello. It's me Jack." He poked his head inside.

"Come in, Jack," Patty said.

Digging his hands deep into his pockets, he rocked back on his heels. There, sitting quietly was Ashton, watching something on the television. "This is nice," he said, tipping his head toward his son.

"He loves this show. We turn it on, and he won't move a muscle until it's over with. The best babysitter since a little shot of bourbon in the bottle." Lilly snickered.

"Now, now, Lilly. I'm sure you never put any alcohol in Annie's or Mary's bottle," Jack said.

"No, of course not. But their father, well, that's another story." She cackled, making Ashton look away from the television.

"Daddy," he said, running and jumping into Jack's arms.

"Ready for dinner?"

"I'm hungry," he said.

"You ladies joining us tonight?" Jack asked as he stepped back out of the tiny living area.

"We were going to. But I think we'll just stay in. We have some canned soup here, and some crackers. We'll be fine," Lilly said, getting up from the sofa.

"Tell Annie we'll take a raincheck." Patty patted Jack on the arm while leaning in for a kiss from Ashton. "Sweet boy. We love you," she sang.

"If you need anything just holler. We're just next door." Jack smiled.

"Yes, Jack, we know." Lilly furrowed her brows.

Jack turned his back on them and began to head out. He came to a halt, turning around. "You know you two are welcome to come over any time. You don't need an invitation. The door is always open."

"That's so sweet of you to say, Jack," Patty said.

"We know you've been at work all day and would like to spend some time with your beautiful wife and family. You don't need us old broads over all the time," Lilly said.

"I don't think of you as old. I'd rather put you in the category of experienced beyond years."

"Patty, that's just a nice way of saying old." Lilly cackled.

"At any rate, you both are welcome to come over any time. That's my story, and I'm sticking to it. By the way, have you noticed anything strange with Annie?"

Both women's eyes bulged then they shook their heads.

"It's probably nothing, but the last couple of nights she's seemed distant."

"I know she's been thinking a lot about the bakery. Should she sell it, should she keep it. That sort of thing," Patty said.

"Okay, as long as it's just that. I didn't want it to be about me. I'm so deep with wood orders I can hardly come up for air."

"I know, dear. She knows it too. I think that's why it's weighing on her so. She wants to be home with the children, but a small part of her is envious about your work. She once felt that way too," Patty said softly. "Just keep talking to her. Don't let her clam up. Us McPherson women tend to keep it all inside.

Jack's jaw dropped.

"Speak for yourself, Patty Bolander," Lilly said, her unabashed tone coming through loud and clear.

Jack laughed. "Good night, you two."

"Good night," they said, waving as he walked out the door.

THE SMELL of basil filled the kitchen. On the stove, the tomato soup sputtered softly. Jack watched as Annie flipped the sandwiches. "Darn, a little brown."

"I like my grilled cheese toasty," Jack said, taking the spatula from her.

Annie moved to the soup pot and began to ladle out the soup. "Grandmother and Auntie not coming?"

"No, they decided to stay in. Something about having soup there." Jack slid the sandwiches off and plated them.

"They've been acting rather strangely. I don't know what's gotten into them." Annie carried the bowls to the table.

Jack knitted his brows. This was weird. He thought she was acting differently. She thought they were acting differently. Maybe he was the one behaving strangely. "How so?" he called out.

"I asked them earlier if they wanted to come over and have tea. They declined. Then they asked if Ashton could come over."

"What's so strange about asking Ashton to come over?" Jack lifted the plate with the grilled cheese and crossed over to the table. He turned to the living area where Ashton was playing with his metal cars.

Annie placed her hands on her hips. "You don't find it strange that eighty-year-old women want to have a four-year-old over?"

"He's almost five. He was fine. You should have seen him. He was enthralled in a television show."

"Did you smell his breath?" Annie asked.

Jack belted out a hearty laugh. "You know about the bourbon, huh?"

"Ashton, dinner is ready," Annie called. "Yes, I know, and they better never do that to our children."

Just then, Carolina opened up her lungs and cried, sending Annie running. "You guys go ahead. I'll be a while."

Jack helped Ashton into his booster chair. He placed half a sandwich on the table. As he watched Ashton lick the cheese that oozed out between the toasty slices of bread, his mind wandered for a brief minute. Were any of the McPherson women telling him straight? Sometimes they could be so hard to read. He clasped his hands, and while in thought, waited for Annie.

"Here you go, changed and ready to see Daddy," Annie said, handing Carolina over.

Jack pulled her up and kissed her on the check. "How's my baby girl today?"

Carolina cooed at her Daddy.

"Sit down and eat. I'll take my turn afterward," Jack said, nodding toward the bowl of soup.

Except for the murmurs coming from the television in the other room, the only other sounds were spoons hitting bowls, slurping sounds, and Ashton slapping the table-topand kicking his feet against the chair legs.

"Everything all right, Annie?" Jack repositioned Carolina in his arms.

"Yes, why do you ask? In fact, that's the second time

tonight you've asked that same question." She peered at him through half-closed lids.

"I just sense something is bothering you, is all. I hope you know you can tell me anything."

"Of course," Annie said, dipping her spoon in the bowl. "I guess I do have a lot on my mind." She set the spoon down into the soup, letting it rest on the side of the bowl.

"What kind of things on your mind?" He lifted his right brow and waited.

"What should I do with the bakery. Sell it, lease it out, run it, or something else?"

"Those are all viable options," he said.

She sighed.

"What do you want to do?"

"Part of me misses working there. I started that business from the ground up, you know."

He let out a chuckle. "Yes, dear, I do know."

"I want more bread," Ashton yelled.

"Use your inside voice," Jack said.

Tossing a quarter of grilled cheese onto his tray, he sat back down.

"I want juice," Ashton screamed.

Annie could feel the vein in her neck bulging. "Now, that's enough, Ashton."

"I think he wants attention," Jack said, giving Ashton a sharp look.

Annie set the sippy cup full of milk on his tray. He immediately put it to his mouth. He spit it out. "Juice," he demanded.

"You're having milk, young man. Drink it, or have nothing," Jack said, scolding him.

Ashton threw his head back and wailed.

Jack handed Carolina over to Annie and whisked Ashton out of the chair so fast, Ashton gulped a wad of air and started coughing.

Looking over his shoulder, he made eye contact with Annie. "We'll be right back."

Annie bounced Carolina on one knee while she finished eating her dinner. This was becoming the norm around Magnolia. How could she ever think she could go back to work?

The sounds of Ashton's little shoes as he ran across the wood floor caused her to look up.

"I'm sorry," he said, holding out his arms.

Annie caught Jack's gaze.

"Okay, I accept your apology. Do you want to finish your dinner?"

He nodded.

Jack picked him up and got him settled back on the booster seat.

Facing Annie, he clasped his hands in front, resting them on the table. "Now, where were we?"

"Ha ha. Right. We were discussing the demise of Sweet Indulgence." She lowered her head.

"Demise? No, we were talking about maybe you going back to work. I think it's a great idea."

Raising her head, she locked her eyes on him. "You do? But the children are so young. They need their mommy." Her eyes teared up when she looked at them.

"Maybe part-time is the answer?" Jack said.

Shaking her head, she stood.

"Just think about it. Whatever you decide, I'm here for you. We can make anything work."

Reaching over, she began gathering dishes while still holding Carolina. Jack jumped up and took them out of her hand. "I got this. Why don't you go sit in the living room, put your feet up? I'll wash up Ashton and the dishes. Maybe Daddy will put Ashton in the sink with all the sudsy water." He leaned over and nuzzled Ashton's nose, making him laugh. "No, Daddy." His laughter infectious, soon, all of them were in stitches, even baby Carolina.

"By the way, I passed Vicky and Scott on their way to the airport tonight. They have a long flight," Jack said.

Annie moved toward the living room. "Yes, I hope

everything works out for them, and they bring little Jackson home safe and sound."

"Jasmine," Ashton called out.

"Yes, Jasmine is going to have a brother. His name is Jackson," Annie said.

Fluffing up the couch pillows, Annie settled into the soft cushions, still holding Carolina. She loved the baby age, but she also loved when they became a little more independent too. Soon she'd be crawling, followed by walking, and then becoming this little person with opinions, gestures, and ideas. Just like Ashton. Annie widened her eyes, letting her jaw drop. "Just like Ashton." A small chuckle came from nowhere. "Please, not quite as strong-willed as Ashton."

CHAPTER 10

Wetting a paper towel, he wiped Ashton's mouth, dusted off the crumbs, and set him down. "Time for a bath, big guy," Jack said, taking him by the hand.

"I'll do that, hon," Annie said when she got wind of what he was up to.

"No, you stay put. I'll have him in and out in a jiffy."

Annie warmed up some baby food and fed Carolina. "This teamwork stuff works well," she said to herself. By the time she finished feeding Carolina, Ashton was done with his bath and dressed in his pajamas.

"The kitchen is sparkling. Thank you," she said, posing for a kiss.

He obliged her, kissing her softly. "You're welcome."

"Kids are fed, bathed, and soon off to bed. How

grateful I am to have such a loving and thoughtful husband."

"Well, I have to admit, I'd like to spend some alone time with my beautiful wife." He winked.

"Oh, I see," she said, teasing him with her flirty look.

"You put Carolina to bed, and I'll put Ashton in bed." He grabbed his son's hand and practically pulled him down the hall.

Annie's heart melted. This man. She loved him so much.

Ashton looked back with a stunned look. Annie snickered. "I'll be right there to kiss you good night."

They met in the hallway, passing by Ashton's bedroom and waltzing into Carolina's. She watched as he leaned over the crib, caressing his baby girl's head. She stepped into Ashton's room, decorated with dinosaurs, and found him cuddled under the blanket. "Daddy didn't read me a story tonight."

She knew he wanted his alone time with her, but reading a bedtime story was like the best thing you could do for a kid. She picked a book from the shelf and began to read it.

"Mommy. Slow down. You missed a part."

Nothing could get by this kid. Not even speed reading. She started over.

Clicking off the light, she said good night and then

gently closed the door, leaving a crack open. Moving down the hall, she came to an abrupt halt. What was that noise? She crept closer to the living room. There, spread out on the sofa was Jack, his bottom lip shaking, his eyes fluttering, and an awful sound coming out of his mouth. Putting her hands on her hips, she smiled down at the man she loved. "A for effort, Jack Powell. A for effort," she whispered.

"SORRY ABOUT LAST NIGHT, BABE." Jack poured coffee into his travel mug.

"No problem. I know you were tired. You must be with all the orders you've been getting."

"We need to continue our conversation tonight." He pulled her in and kissed her.

"Conversation? Was that what we were going to do last night?"

He smiled back at her. "I mean about Sweet Indulgence. The rest of it, well, it can come after." He grabbed his lunch box out of the fridge.

"Have a good day," she called to him.

"I love you," he yelled as he went out the door.

"I love you too," she said, albeit a bit late after the door closed.

ANNIE'S DAY began and ended the same each day. Feed the children, straighten up the house, toss a load of clothes into the washing machine, chase Ashton around, and then repeat. Her only rest came when they both went down for a nap. She vowed to take that time to do something just for her. But, alas, it never came to be. Instead, she'd sit on the sofa, feet propped up on the coffee table, sipping a cup of warmed tea, occasionally closing her eyes and listening for any noise, but mostly just enjoying having her arms free, and the silence of the house to soothe her. That and the cup of tea.

She'd set her phone on vibrate. Any noise could change the dynamics, throwing out the quietness she enjoyed, and she wasn't risking it for anything. She didn't recognize the number flashing on her screen.

"Hello?"

"Annie. This is Robert."

"Robert. I didn't recognize the number. Is everything all right?"

"Can you get someone to watch the children? You're needed at the hospital."

His voice was eerily calm, and instead of it reassuring her, the opposite occurred.

"What's happened to Jack?" Her tone elevated in pitch with each word.

"I'LL CALL you and let you know what's happened. I don't have any details," Annie said, rushing around the house.

"It's going to be fine, dear. Slow down. Take a deep breath," Auntie Patty said.

"Annie, we'll take good care of the children. You go be with Jack. Call us right away," Grandmother Lilly said.

"I didn't even have time to shower today. I was just sitting on the couch, enjoying the quietness of the house," she said as she tried to contain her emotion.

"You look fine," Auntie said, wiping a smudge of something off her cheek. "Put on a coat. It's chilly out."

"I wish Vicky was here to help. They flew to Korea," Annie said, tears welling up and trailing down her cheek.

"We'll be fine. We've taken care of children before. Go. Drive safely," Lilly said.

Annie bolted out the door and jumped into her car. She didn't even remember the drive to MUSC, but when she stepped into the emergency room, the reality of where she was hit her like a ton of bricks. She began to make her way to the desk when she spotted Robert and Milly, Jack's parents huddled in a corner. She hurried over to them.

"Where's Jack. What's happened?"

"There's been an accident," Robert said.

"What sort of accident?" Annie asked.

"Machinery," he replied.

"Machinery? Oh my. How bad is it?"

"We're waiting for more word. The ambulance brought him here. There was so much blood, I'm not sure how bad it is, Annie."

Robert spoke softly, but the words he used told Annie that it was anything but a little scratch. This was serious business. She placed her hand over her heart to compress the pain she felt. The tears, now coming down hard, made seeing impossible. She wiped them away with the back of her hand. Milly offered her a Kleenex.

Sliding her arm around Annie's shoulders, she squeezed her. "Jack is tough. He'll pull through. We just have to be here for him."

Annie couldn't catch her breath. She sobbed uncontrollably. The unknown was the worst.

With her eyes blurry and her mind a million miles away, Annie didn't even notice the man with the stethoscope around his neck approaching them.

"Are you Jack Powell's family?"

The three of them stood. "I'm his wife. What's happened. Can I see him?"

The doctor placed his hand on her shoulder and guided her to sit. When Robert and Milly followed suit, he sat too.

"He's sedated right now. We're getting him ready for surgery."

Gasps came from all of them.

Annie cried into her hands. Milly rubbed her back as she repeated over and over, oh dear, oh dear.

"Doctor, what can you tell us to help ease our concerns?" Robert said.

"I can tell you his vitals are good. He's a strong young man, healthy, and we feel he will make a full recovery."

"A full recovery from what?" Annie said, her brows furrowed.

"We won't know until the surgeon gets in there, but there's a possibility Jack will lose his hand."

"His hand!" Annie wailed.

"I'm sorry. That's all I can say right now. Why don't you go to the third-floor waiting room? They'll come out and discuss everything with you after his surgery."

"Annie," Mary yelled as she came dashing toward her.

"What happened to Jack?" Danny said, out of breath.

"He's going in for surgery. He may lose his hand." Annie rested her head on Mary's shoulder and cried.

Rearing her head up quickly and pushing away from Mary, she wiped her tears. "The kids. They're with Grandmother and Auntie. Vicky is out of the country. Can you please go and relieve them?"

"Of course. Whatever you need," Mary said, her gaze darting from Danny to Annie.

"Yes. We'll go hold down the fort, but you must keep us posted," Danny said.

"We'll stay with Annie," Milly said.

"How'd the accident occur?" Danny said.

"He was using some fancy new piece of equipment he got. I guess it cut him. The doctors are going to try and save his hand, but we just don't know. There was so much blood," Robert said, shaking his head, clearly traumatized by the events.

Danny and Mary took off to Magnolia to care for the children. Robert and Milly took Annie to the third floor, where they served her coffee and snacks from the vending machines.

"You must eat something to keep up your strength. Jack is going to need you," Milly said, handing her a bag of beef jerky.

"He's been so busy with orders. Then he comes home

to two rambunctious children and a wife who isn't the most cheerful. No wonder he had an accident."

"Now, Annie, don't blame yourself. Jack loves you all so much." Milly patted Annie's hand.

"Jack worships you and the children, Annie. He loves his job, working with his hands, seeing the final product, and when the customers rave about it, it just makes it that much better. He's told me on more than one occasion that it was you that was instrumental in him getting his company off the ground. He wants you to be happy too. He's told me as much," Robert said, his bottom lip quivering just a bit, the emotion seeping out, even in him.

Annie hung her head.

Taking his finger, he gently lifted her chin. "Annie. Seriously. Don't beat yourself up about this accident. We'll cope with it the way any family handles tragedy. Head on. We will see it through, and no matter what, Jack will survive whatever he is dealt. I know that much."

"He's the love of my life. I can't let anything happen to him. The kids and I need him."

"He's not going anywhere, Annie," Robert said, pulling her close.

The next couple of hours were pure torture for them as they sat around waiting for word from the doctor. It was a pretty somber place to be. Low cries, red eyes, people holding hands and offering support filled the area. The halls echoed with shoes as hospital staff made their rounds. Soft voices and an occasional laugh could be heard as people passed through. Annie found nothing funny about being there. But to be fair, life went on for those who worked there, and she couldn't hold them responsible for enjoying a joke or two. A small chuckle escaped her mouth when she recalled Ashton's latest challenge—trying to get a box of animal crackers off the kitchen counter. He opened the cabinet, stepped inside on the shelf, and then gripping the counter, pulled himself up so he could see the box. But he couldn't figure out how to get them and stay hold of the counter. Frustrated, he dropped down only to miss the shelf and came tumbling onto the floor. Not hurt, only his ego bruised, he sighed and then asked for help.

Hugging her arms, she smiled. There was always something to be thankful for, something to smile about. Her children and her husband always made her happy.

"Mrs. Powell?"

"Yes. I'm Annie Powell."

A warm hand shook hers. "I'm Doctor Hernandez. I did the surgery on Jack's hand."

"How is he? Can I see him?"

"Yes, he's waking up in the recovery room. I'm sorry, but we weren't able to save his hand."

The words bounced around in her brain, but she

couldn't catch any of them long enough to make out what they meant.

"He's very lucky. It could have been his entire arm. He has some physical therapy to do to get things going again with the use of his arm. His shoulder was dislocated as well. But he's a strong young man, and I expect not having a hand will not slow him down in the least."

Closing her eyes, a rush of warm sensation came over her, bringing with it a slight ringing in her ears. Her body began to sway, followed by numbness of her limbs, and then down on the floor she went.

CHAPTER 11

"What happened?" Annie looked up to see Milly standing over her.

"You fainted," Milly said.

"I did? I don't think I've ever done that before," she said, trying to sit up.

"Take it easy, sport," Robert said. "There's no rush to get up."

His warm smile put her at ease. Letting her head slowly down to the pillow, she sighed. "Jack? Any word on Jack?"

"We've been in to see him. He's in good spirits. He wants to see you, but we told him you'd had a little setback," Robert said.

Annie rubbed her forehead with the palm of her hand.

"I'm supposed to be the strong one for him, not the other way around. Of all the times to faint."

"You hadn't eaten. They said your blood sugar was low. You're going to be fine, and so is Jack," Milly said.

"How bad is it? Tell me now."

"It's all wrapped up tightly right now. But what the doctor explained to us was he did lose his hand to the wrist. Fortunately for him, it was his left hand since he's right-handed," Robert said.

"How's he going to be able to continue with his wood business?" Annie closed her eyes.

"He'll find a way. If I know anything about Jack Powell, it's that he's resourceful. He'll not let this accident stop him. It may slow him down a bit at first, but mark my words, Annie. He'll come back fighting."

Annie watched as Robert turned away. He tried to conceal his emotion, but when his hand flew up and wiped the tears, it was a dead giveaway.

"I'm stepping out for some air."

"Is he going to be okay?" Annie asked.

"Yes. Listen, the doctor said Jack is completely aware of his condition and seemed to take it in stride. He's on pain pills so he can't feel anything right now. He'll need physical therapy for sure, and maybe even some other therapies to help him get through this, but the important thing we all must drive home is that we're here for him, to support him however."

Annie saw Milly's look of sheer determination as she told her how things would be. For the first time ever, she realized where Jack got his tenacity. His mother.

"Please find a doctor or nurse. I want to get out of this bed and go see my husband." Annie showed Milly that she too could be firm if need be.

"I'M JUST FINE. This is ridiculous that I have to be wheeled in. I ate some food, drank some water. I'm not light-headed at all. Please let me walk into Jack's room on my two feet."

"Doctor's orders," the nurse said, pushing her.

Robert took the lead when they reached Jack's room and pushed open the door. Milly followed behind him, then the nurse pushed Annie in. Jack was sleeping.

"Honey," Annie said, rubbing his arm softly.

His eyes fluttered.

"Babe. It's me. Annie," she whispered.

A soft moan escaped his lips.

"He's probably drowsy still from the meds," the nurse said.

"Jack. Dad here."

"Mom is here too," Milly chirped.

Annie picked up his right hand and kissed it, being careful to avoid the needle that was pumping meds into him.

"Hi," Jack said, barely audible.

"Honey. I'm here. I'm sorry I wasn't here earlier. I had a little mishap."

"Fainted," he mumbled, then sighed.

"Yes. I guess the news about—"

"Son," Robert said, interrupting her. "Would you like us to open the blinds a bit and let some sunshine in? Or how about I turn on the television and see if I can find something to bore you with." He chuckled.

Milly shook her head at Annie, then put her finger to her lips. Annie figured it out quickly. She wasn't to speak of the accident yet.

"The kids are with Mary and Danny."

"Good," he said.

"You're not in any pain, right?" Annie asked.

He moved his head side to side.

"Hello, Powell family," the doctor said as he came into the room.

Everyone looked his way.

He moved to Jack's side. Taking out his stethoscope, he listened to Jack's heart, followed by feeling his pulse.

He looked at the bandaged stump and then made eye contact with Jack.

"Everything is good. Your bandage looks great, your vitals are perfect. I'd like to keep you overnight and see how things are in the morning. We don't keep patients in hospital beds long these days, but instead, schedule follow-ups and physical therapy right away. I'll get the orthopedic surgeon to come in and do his assessment before we discharge him, but if things go as they have, I would think Jack can go home tomorrow, early evening. We'll just have to see how things go. Any questions?"

"Tomorrow? That soon? I mean...that's great news. I know he'd be more comfortable at Magnolia, but are we ready for him? What do I need to do?" Annie stopped herself from rattling on.

"As part of his discharge, you'll be given a complete list of do's and don'ts. I think he's going to be okay with some modifications as he becomes used to his injury. I'll get his plan going, and then you'll feel more comfortable with the discharge."

"Thank you, Doctor," Robert said.

Milly put her arm around Annie.

"Thank you," Annie muttered.

"Can I have a few moments with Jack alone?" Annie locked eyes with Milly.

Robert clasped Milly's hand and led her outside the room.

"Jack. Can you hear me?"

He opened his eyes. "Yes. I'm still a bit groggy."

"Groggy is okay. I can understand you clearly. I think you're coming around."

"I love you," she said.

"Love you too. Ashton, Carolina?"

"They're with Mary and Danny, remember?"

"That's right. You did say that."

She was happy he remembered that. Surely that was a good sign.

"Grandmother and Auntie were helping me out with the kids, but I sent in the rescue squad." She laughed, hoping to spawn at least a smile out of him. And it worked.

"Yeah because they can be a handful."

"We're going to get through this, Jack. It's just a temporary setback. You wait and see. There's not going to be anything you can't do."

"Setback. Like your fainting?" He turned his head slightly and smiled at her.

"Right. Like my fainting."

He closed his eyes.

"Jack, I'm going to go now. You rest. I'll be back tomorrow to bring you home."

"Annie," he whispered.

"Yes, Jack." She dropped back down to the chair and touched his arm.

"Next time you want attention, try something else besides fainting." The gleam from his eye bounced right to her.

A small tear bobbled on her lower lid. She answered with a hint of a smile on her face. "I'll keep that in mind." She leaned over and kissed him.

She'd totally forgotten she'd been wheeled into the room until Milly's jaw dropped and pointed to her legs.

Waving off her response, Annie insisted all was well. "I'm good. Thanks for your concern."

The three of them walked to the parking garage in silence. So many things were going through her mind. Like how would she tell Ashton, or how would Jack do once he was home. It was all a bit too surreal to sort it all out.

"Call us when you get home. The traffic is going to be awful with all the commuters," Robert said.

"I'll take my time. I'll be fine."

Milly kissed her cheek. "Stay strong," she said, stepping back.

Annie nodded.

Robert slid his hand up her forearm and then held it in

place. "She's right. Stay strong for Jack and for the little guy at home. He's going to have a lot of questions."

"I've been tossing around how to tell him." She lowered her gaze.

"You tell him Daddy had an accident with a powerful tool. He hurt his hand pretty badly, and they had to do surgery. I'm sure Jack will have the bandage on for quite a while. As time goes on, Jack will find a way to explain it all to him. Right now, you go home, hug those grand-children for us, and try to get some rest. Would you like us to meet you here tomorrow?" Milly asked.

"Sure. That would be great."

Once inside her car, Annie took several deep breaths. Closing her eyes, she counted to ten and then ran through the alphabet, trying to ward off any emotional outburst that may come with having time to take it in. Grieving for Jack. No tears came, just the sounds of her heavy breath-ing. She set the radio for some soothing music and took to the roads which would lead her to home sweet home.

"MOMMY," Ashton said, running into her arms.

"Hey, baby," Annie said, hugging him close, kissing the top of his head.

She peered over his little head and saw Mary and Danny standing together, a look of sadness in their eyes.

"I let him stay up when you called and said you were on the way home. He's been asking a lot of questions," Mary said, tipping her head.

"Sure, that's fine. How's Carolina?"

"Sleeping. She took a bottle and went down without a fuss."

"I'm exhausted. I think I'll get this guy to bed and hop in the shower."

"Can we talk to you for a moment?" Danny asked.

The three of them walked into the other room.

"So, spell it out. How bad is it?" Danny locked eyes with her.

"Anytime you have a trauma to a limb where surgery is required, it's serious. He's lost his hand. His left hand, but still…"

"How is he doing? Is he depressed, sad, what are his emotions right now?" Mary said.

"Mary, it just happened. How in the world would I know this? He seems like Jack. He didn't even mention it to me. It didn't even come up in our conversation. I told him we love him and will support him. But I don't know the total ramifications of this."

"He's being released tomorrow, though?" Danny asked.

"Tentatively. It will depend on a few things. I'm hopeful."

Mary opened up her arms. "Come here, Sis."

Her legs felt like stone pillars. Putting one foot in front of the other, she shuffled forward, taking more effort than she'd expected. Finally reaching her, Annie rested her head on Mary's shoulder, then proceeded to weep like a baby.

Mary patted her back, trying to console her. "Now, now, Annie. Everything is going to be all right."

CHAPTER 12

*N*o one said it would be easy, just that he'd learn to live with his new disability. Anytime there is a bump in the road, it causes a little stress. Annie convinced herself of that, but more importantly, she tried to convince Jack. So when he'd try to reach for something with that hand, or pick something up and it became awkward, Annie reassured Jack this was just a learning curve. When four-letter words flew out of his mouth, though, Annie pretended the frustration she heard wasn't for real. It was a coping mechanism she used for a lot of things in her life.

"Here, let me help you with that, Jack."

He whirled away and then stomped off, leaving her standing, her jaw dropping.

"Jack, come back. I was—"

"I know what you were doing. You were babying me…again!" He waved her off and kept walking.

She picked up the broken pieces of the plate and tossed them into the garbage pail. Suddenly, Carolina began to cry in the other room, sending Annie in another direction, almost forgetting about the spat she and Jack just had.

Hearing the door slam and right after, Ashton, who'd been content on the sofa watching television, let out a loud, "Daddy, where are you going," prompted Annie to quickly draw Carolina up into her arms and rush out to the living room. Jack was gone. She picked up the pace and opened the front door. She watched his frame sway as he raced out of her view. He was headed down to the dock. The sky was gray, and the trees, mostly bare now except for the stately Magnolia tree where they'd buried their time capsule at the trunk, showed all the signs winter was upon them. The bleakness of the landscape dived into her soul and muddied her spirit. Give her a day of sunshine, and no matter what, her mood radiated like feet dipped into warm sand.

She turned and went back inside, defeated. She had to give him space.

Ashton sat on his new booster seat up at the big people's table, nibbling on small pieces of vegetables as Annie finished getting dinner ready. She peered at the clock on the stove. Jack had been gone for three hours. Dusk was about to arrive, and Annie knew that even though Lady Powell was equipped with lights, it wasn't safe for him to be out on the water at night, alone. Annie wondered if she'd feel differently had he not been injured.

She'd placed the bowl of macaroni and cheese in front of Ashton, then turned to Carolina, who now was using Ashton's highchair.

"Sister is in my chair," he said in between bites.

"Yes, she is. Thank you for sharing it with her." Annie slid the spoon into the jar and whirled it around. They'd kept him in a highchair way too long. Or maybe they wanted to baby Carolina longer. Either way, Annie was feeling a bit blue about all the changes going on. Annie's own tummy began to growl, but she didn't have time to eat. She was worried sick about Jack while trying to conceal her angst from the children. She'd read some-where they could sense stress and turmoil. She was so good at covering things up.

All heads turned or looked up when Jack came through the front door. Ashton yelled out, Carolina made some noise, and Annie held her breath a moment too long before letting it escape. She wanted to give him space. Not baby him.

"There's macaroni and cheese on the stove if you're

hungry," Annie said, turning her attention back to Carolina.

"I'm not hungry. I'm going to take a shower and then hit the hay."

"It's a little early to go to bed, isn't it? I mean, the kids would like to see you." She searched for words of confidence and comfort, but nothing came.

"Now you're going to tell me when I'm sleepy or not? Please, Annie. Get over yourself."

Annie's lids slowly closed, but a few tears leaked out before she could hide them.

"Mommy's crying," Ashton said, puckering out his lower lip.

"Mommy is fine. Finish your dinner," she whispered.

Annie couldn't ward off the hunger pangs any longer and finally broke down and warmed up a bowl of the mac and cheese. Ashton and Carolina were playing nicely in the living room. He was showing her his cars and trucks. Everything was okay until she put one bite in her mouth.

"Mommy, Carolina is slobbering all over my toys!"

"Ashton, she's a baby. That's what they do. Let me remind you, you were a baby once too. You put all sorts of things in your mouth. Dirt, rocks, even dog poop. Well, not really. Daddy got the dog poop out of your hand before you ate it." She crossed her arms and smirked.

"Yuck! Buffy or Isla?"

"It doesn't matter. It was dog poop!"

With the mention of their names, both dogs raised up. When they realized it was nothing, they snuggled back down into the giant-sized bed they shared.

Annie checked her watch. It was bath time. She made a mad dash to the bathroom and began to fill the tub. She stepped out into the hall and looked down at their bedroom door. It was closed. She gazed toward the living room, both kids were still playing nice. She turned off the water and grabbed pajamas for Ashton.

"Bath time, Ashton." She leaned over and picked up Carolina.

While Ashton played in the tub, she sat on the closed toilet seat and bounced Carolina on her knee. Jack normally helped her with the whole nighttime routine, but he went to bed. She supposed Ashton could have skipped his bath, but Annie was trying to make everything as normal as she could.

After she got both kids in bed, she read Ashton a story. He didn't like the fact that Jack wasn't reading it to him, but finally, he gave in. Annie closed the book when she'd read the last word. "You know, Ashton, Daddy is still recovering from his hurt hand. We need to be patient with him as it heals."

"Yes, Mommy. But will he be my daddy still?"

Annie put the book on the table. "Of course, he'll be your daddy still."

"He's not playing with me anymore."

Annie rolled in her lips and bit down.

"I miss him," he said, crying crocodile tears.

Even though they were fake tears, she believed he was sad. He just didn't know how to express it. "I know you do. Just give it some more time." She dropped a kiss on his forehead. "Good night."

"Good night, Mommy. I love you."

"I love you more."

She poured herself a glass of wine and sipped on it in the dark. How much longer would they be able to live like this? Granted, it'd only been a month, but she was hoping he'd be stronger than this. He'd never let anything defeat him as long as she had known him. Jack Powell was one tough cookie. So why did she feel so exposed and alone?

CHAPTER 13

*C*reeping into the bedroom so as not to wake him, Annie moved to the bathroom to get ready for bed. She tried to make as little noise as possible. But no doubt the noise from her toothbrush as it swept over her teeth and the gargling noise following resonated to the other room. She switched off the light and tiptoed to her side of the bed. Lying there, snoring, Jack hadn't moved a muscle since she first came into the room. Pulling the covers back on her side, she slid under. Lying on her back, she listened to the rhythm of his breathing while looking up to a dark ceiling, a soft glow of the moon peeping in through the blinds the only light, and wondered if this was the new them, or just a temporary roadblock. Suddenly he snorted, rolled over on his side, mumbled something, and continued snoring.

The next morning, she awoke to an empty bed. Her heart raced. Jack. Where was he? Stumbling out of her sleeping stupor, she didn't even take the time to wash the sleep from her eyes but moved quickly down the hall. About halfway, she heard giggles and the low, deep voice of her husband. A cheery ring to his tone made her smile. A new day, a new Jack.

"Good morning," she said, pulling her straggly hair back away from her face.

"Good morning, Mommy. Daddy made pancakes."

She whiffed in the aroma of warm maple syrup. "I see that. Daddy makes yummy pancakes."

"Coffee?" Jack asked as he moved toward the Keurig.

"In a bit. I just woke up. You were gone, and I got concerned."

"Concerned? Because I wasn't in the bed?" His cheery tone suddenly turned condescending.

"Jack. Don't," she pleaded, nodding toward Ashton.

He harrumphed then made a second cup for himself. "I'm taking the boat out today, and Ashton is going with me," he announced.

Annie had checked on the forecast the night before and knew that they were expecting cold, wind, and possibly rain. Not exactly the best boating weather. She wondered what he was trying to prove. She gulped, pausing before answering.

"Not today, Jack. The weatherman says the weather is going to be bad."

"And the weatherman knows best for me and my son?"

Annie's gaze settled on Ashton. His little eyes were bouncing back and forth from his dad to her, waiting to see who was going to win this battle.

"Can I see you for a moment. In the bedroom." She turned and walked away.

She peeked in on Carolina as she made her way back to the bedroom. She was awake, but content. She knew she'd only have a few minutes before her contentment turned sour.

"Jack, what are you trying to prove?

"That we Powell men are strong, and nothing can stop us from doing something if we want it badly enough," he said, his tone traveling an octave or two.

"Why don't you start by showing him how to respect his mom. You trying to talk over me, make decisions without me will not bode well for you. I can promise you that." She peered at him through half-closed lids, seething mad inside he'd push her to say these things.

"Oh, now I don't respect women. Please." He waved her off.

"Jack. What's happening to us? You're not the same man I married. I want Jack Powell back. The guy who walked into my bakery six years ago and swept me off my feet. The guy with the dimples that made me burn up with desire every time you flashed your smile. I want Ashton's playful daddy back, and Carolina's favorite teddy bear. I want you back just as before." A tear tumbled down her cheek.

He bowed his head. "I can never be that same guy to you or to them."

She lifted his chin with her finger and stared into his eyes. "Why?"

"I'm not one hundred percent anymore." He held up his wrapped stump.

"Jack, that doesn't matter to us. It could have been so much worse. Yes, I understand it's been awkward for you to learn to do things with one hand, but I have to tell you, you've done brilliantly. The kids and I love you just as you are, and when we made our vows, I said in sickness and health. You said it too. And you've been there for me when I went through postpartum depression after Ashton's birth, and you've been by my side while I battle the do's and don'ts of being a small businesswoman. Don't you think I'd stand by you in your time of need?"

She wasn't expecting what happened next. He balled up his hands, tossed his head back in anger and yelled. Then, he crumbled to the floor into a fetal position, sobbing. She fell to her knees and cradled his head in her arms and wept with him too. She prayed this was the turning point for them. He'd see she was there for him and let her in. She rocked him while saying over and over, "I love you, Jack, and we'll get through this."

She was so emotionally connected with Jack and what was happening she didn't hear the patter of little feet come in.

"Mommy, is everything okay with Daddy?"

Annie held her hand out to him. "Yes, baby. Come here."

Jack rolled up to a sitting position, quickly wiping away his tears. "Hey, champ. I'm okay." He winked at Annie.

Carolina began to fuss, getting all their attention.

"You get Carolina, Ashton and I will make some fresh pancakes. Come on, buddy." He jumped up, taking Ashton by the hand and leading him down to the kitchen.

Annie couldn't move despite Carolina wailing in the other room. It was all too surreal, this moment, and as suddenly as the crisis began, it was as suddenly over. She held on to the edge of the bed as she pulled herself up, her legs wobbly, her heart still racing from seeing Jack collapse. Drawing in a deep breath, she counted to ten and then ran through the alphabet, a calming exercise she happened upon that seemed to work for her. Steadying her body, she put one foot in front of the other and made it to Carolina's room. In the other part of the house, she could hear her two favorite guys banging pans and laughing. Maybe, just maybe, Jack Powell had his moment. The one when he realized they'd all be there for him, even in his gloomiest moments, and now, seeing the positive side of their love and support, the light at the end of the tunnel shone bright, leading the way out of the darkness.

Clearly still unsure of how to proceed, Annie and Carolina entered the kitchen to find Jack flipping pancakes, and little Ashton setting the table. He was tall for his age, so he could see over the table, and with his tongue secured between his teeth, Annie witnessed him painstakingly making sure everything was just so.

"You're doing such a great job, buddy," Jack said.

"He sure is," Annie said, announcing they'd arrived.

"Just in time for some hot pancakes," he said, whirling around, making eye contact and smiling. "How's my baby girl?" He moved toward Carolina and tickled her.

Annie secured Carolina in her highchair, moving toward the cabinet where the cups were stored. Their routine was eerily normal, and she didn't know what to say or do. Would it just be a matter of minutes or hours when Jack would have another meltdown?

Jack busily stacked the pancakes and walked over to

the table. "I was wondering about our annual Christmas get-together. I realized I messed up Thanksgiving, but there's no reason to postpone Christmas."

It was true. Halloween and Thanksgiving were both blurs. They'd normally celebrate Jack's birthday with a big costume party. Thanksgiving was always a blast whenever you got the entire family together. And now Christmas was just three weeks away. She knew the family would come, but they usually had a big open house and invited friends they hadn't seen all year too. Just because everyone was so busy.

"I think it's important we have some sort of celebration. You never know when Grandmother and Auntie won't be here."

"True. Let me make some phone calls. I'd love to have Scott and Vicky come, bring the children. I've only seen little Jackson once since they brought him home from Korea," she said, feeling the joy of the holidays already.

"I'll start gathering wood and get it all chopped so we can have a huge bon—"

Annie held her breath and paused. Jack had that deer in the headlights look, and she didn't know how to maneuver around it. The room became so quiet you could hear a pin drop, and except for the thumping of her heart, the silence was deafening.

"Jack," she started.

"I guess I already forgot about this," he said, holding up his arm.

"You've managed to overcome a lot without that hand." She nodded toward the stump.

"Chopping wood might be a bit more difficult. In fact, anything to do with wood might be. I've been thinking about closing up shop."

Here was the other shoe, dropping from high elevation.

"Jack, it's too early to say that, hon. One day at a time."

"We need money, Annie. Income to keep this place going." His tone hitched then lowered.

"We have some income coming in, Jack. And soon you'll be receiving disability payments. It just takes time. We've been saving for a rainy day. We'll just use some of our mad money," she said, trying to make a joke of the terse situation.

"Mad money? That's kind of ironic, isn't it?" His eyes grew dark and scary, causing Annie to shiver.

"You know what I meant by that. It was our vacation money, adding stuff to the house money. Honey," she said, reaching out to him.

Pulling away, he snickered. "So now you're

reminding me that we have to use our life's savings to pull us out of financial despair."

"Jack Powell. Stop it. I realize this is difficult for you. It's difficult for all of us. I'm going back to work," she blurted.

"When were you going to tell me that?" He crossed his arms.

"Jack, not now. The kids." She tipped her chin toward the two with sticky syrup running down their faces.

"I'm going for a walk," he said, storming out of the room.

Closing her eyes, she recited the ABC's again. After she ran through them once, she ran through them again.

CHAPTER 14

*a*nnie finished up cleaning the kitchen, but Jack still hadn't returned from his walk. There were plenty of hours of daylight and even the sun decided to make an appearance, easing her mind some. She got the kids settled into playing while she made several phone calls to friends and family about a holiday party. Every time she contacted someone, they wanted to know first how he was doing, and then what could they bring to the party. By the time she'd finished making the last call, she had a confirmed list of twenty. Hopefully, that would put a smile on Jack's face.

Four hours went by, and now she began to worry. Temperatures were dropping, and in a couple more hours, dusk would be knocking on the door. She tried to recall if he grabbed a coat before rushing out. Pacing the floors, peering out windows, she finally couldn't wait any longer. Bundling up the children, she headed outside.

Pulling the wagon around the property, pretending they were hunting for pine cones, Annie kept one eye out for Jack. As they explored the grounds, stopping only to pick up pine cones, she finally spotted him sitting on a stump, looking out toward the marsh side of their property.

He had to have heard Carolina laughing and Ashton calling his name, but he didn't turn around. She pulled the wagon up close, letting the lever fall to the ground.

"Jack."

"Daddy."

"Jack. Please."

"It's so pretty out here, isn't it?" he said calmly.

Annie rushed to his side, touching his arm softly. "You're scaring me, Jack," she whispered.

"I'm scaring myself," he said, then chuckled.

"It's not funny. I love you. We love you." She choked up.

"I'm going to start seeing the therapist again," he announced.

"Okay. That's good. Whatever you need," she said.

The children were sitting in the wagon, not moving an inch. It broke her heart they were going through this too.

"Would it be all right for me to go to the therapist with you?"

"I'd like that," he said, lacing his arm with hers.

"The children are excited about Christmas. I had an idea. Let's go find a tree. We'll go to our favorite tree farm and pick out the best tree ever. Just like old times. It'll be fun."

He turned his neck toward her, his eyes watering. "I'd like that. Lights and ornaments, with the house decorated, always makes me feel good inside."

Jack pulled the wagon back home while Annie brought up the rear. He laughed with the kids, even jogged a little, giving them a thrill as they went over bumps along the path. When they arrived back at Sweet Magnolia, the house he built with his bare hands, they ascended the stairs together, holding hands, while Ashton ran ahead. Carolina rested on Annie's hip, snuggling against her.

"I made the phone calls. We have twenty confirmed for the party on Christmas Eve."

"Great. Let's go get that tree, then we can plan the menu. Maybe you could help me chop some wood, too, while Grandmother and Auntie watch the kiddos. You know, more bonding time with them." Jack let out a small, fun-loving chuckle and winked.

His chuckle made her smile. "Sure thing. Maybe

Grandmother and Auntie would like to go get the tree with us. Remember last year, they were all about getting the Charlie Brown tree for their cottage."

ANNIE HAD HEARD of people turning over a new leaf, but so quickly? Was this just another short-lived attempt to make her think he was all right, and that suddenly he was learning to live with his disability? She wanted to believe so.

As Annie had suspected, Grandmother and Auntie were excited about tree shopping. They headed to a place they regularly went to. A small gift store filled with one-of-a-kind ornaments, many unique to the Lowcountry, as well as homemade baked goodies like fudge, pecan turtles, and bags of saltwater taffy adorning the shelves. Ashton's eyes widened when he saw the pastel candies tied with colorful ribbons. Annie had decided if he were good during the hunt for the perfect tree, she'd let him pick out some candy and an ornament for the tree.

Jack set off with Ashton, leaving the girls behind. Annie didn't care; she knew they'd eventually catch up.

"Mommy, come here," Ashton yelled, his voice ricocheting.

Annie picked up her pace a bit but didn't want to

leave Grandmother and Auntie too far behind. She could hear them huffing and puffing as it was. She realized it was an effort for them to walk this far, so she slowed it back down a notch.

"Don't wait for us. We'll get there eventually," Grandmother said, her voice catching in between breaths.

Annie made it to the area where Jack and Ashton were. The trees were already cut and tagged, leaning up against a wooden fence. Twirling one around for Annie to inspect, she noticed he was also using his left arm to help guide the tree around.

"I like that one. Seems pretty full, has a nice place to put the star on top. Yes, let's get that one."

Jack held the tree firmly, stomping the trunk on the ground and giving it a good shake. A pine cone came flying off, getting Ashton's attention and lighting up his entire face.

"For our bowl," he said, picking it up and examining it closely.

"Yes, and it's a nice one too."

"Here you are," Auntie Patty said, coming from the path.

"We found the perfect tree," Jack said, holding it out proudly.

"And it didn't take me looking at several. This was the first one he showed me." Annie cocked her head, her mouth turning up at the corners as she lifted her brows.

"Help us find the perfect tree," Grandmother said, grasping Ashton's hand.

The three of them took off among the trees, leaving Jack and Annie behind.

"Annie, I wanted to take a moment while we're alone."

Annie's puzzled look turned worried.

"No, everything is all right. I just wanted to tell you I love you with all of my heart."

"I love you too," she said, taking her time to get the words out.

"I needed a swift kick in the pants, and you gave it to me. I can't sit around and feel sorry for myself. I have a family to feed."

"Jack—"

He held up a finger. "Let me finish."

She nodded.

"It's going to be a bit tight until I can figure some things out. I know you've been on the fence about going back to work at the bakery. If you still want to do that, go ahead. I'll stay home with the kids. When I have a doctor or therapist appointment, I'll ask your grandmother or auntie to help me out, or my mom. She's offered count-less times. I want to spend more time with the children anyway, so this works…that is, if you want to go back to work?"

"Jack, I don't know what to say."

"Just think about it. I know you miss Sweet Indulgence, and I haven't exactly been husband of the year. Going back and rolling up your sleeves will do you good. And, it will give me time with the children." He shrugged.

Ashton came running and smashed into Jack's legs. "Come quick. Grandmother hurt."

Jack let the tree fall behind him and took off running in the direction Ashton had come. Grabbing Ashton's hand, Annie braced Carolina against her side and took off after Jack. The happy moment she'd just shared with Jack drifted away, and guilty thoughts imploded her brain, wondering if the tree finding trip was too much for her elderly family members.

As Annie rounded a corner, she saw Jack bending over and helping Grandmother up. Auntie was laughing hysterically. This didn't seem like an emergency. Grandmother brushed off her pants and shook her head. "I'm such a klutz."

"What happened? Are you hurt?" Annie asked, eyeing Grandmother up and down.

"Just my pride. Ow, and maybe this hip," she said, rubbing it.

"Grandmother. What happened?" Annie demanded.

"She wanted that little tree over there," Auntie Patty said, pointing. "She was being too hardheaded to wait for you guys and decided to go in after it. She lost her balance, and in she went, face first."

"Thanks for wounding my pride again," Lilly said, picking out a piece of pine straw from her mouth.

"Are you sure you're all right? Maybe we should go get an X-ray or something," Jack said, looking for approval from Annie.

Grandmother took a step and winced. All eyes were on her. She took another, this time crying out.

"That's it. We're headed to the hospital to get that hip checked," Annie said.

"I'll go get the car and bring it down the road here."

Jack took off running, leaving them to wait. Soon he brought the car and loaded them all up.

"What about our Christmas tree," Ashton asked, looking back as they drove away.

"We'll have to get it later, sweetie," Annie said, trying to comfort him.

"I've ruined everything," Lilly said.

"No, you didn't. It's going to be fine," Annie said.

"I'll tell you one thing, you gave me a laugh that I won't soon forget," Patty said, trying to conceal her chuckle.

"Oh, you," Lilly said, clearly irritated with her sister. "I'm glad I entertained you."

Jack put the pedal to the metal and got them to the hospital. A feeling of nausea overcame her when she stepped into the emergency room. The same one she visited when Jack got hurt. All the feelings of uncertainty came rushing in. She took a few breaths to ward off another fainting spell. The smells of disinfectant were powerful, and it didn't help to settle her feeling of nausea. They got Grandmother in quickly to see a doctor and get an X-ray.

Now they'd wait for the results.

"YOUR GRANDMOTHER IS A VERY lucky woman. It's not fractured, just bruised," the doctor said.

"Great! Bruised like my ego," Grandmother said.

"I want you to ice it, put heat on it, and take the pain pills. You should be back to yourself in a week or two. As you know, the older we get, the more time it takes to heal."

She waved him off while shuffling to the door. "It will take more than a face-plant with a Christmas tree to bedridden me."

"Hold up. Nurse Palmer, please get us a wheelchair. Mrs. McPherson is ready to go home."

Grandmother started to argue with the nice doctor but realized it was a bad idea, and she'd not win the argument. So as humbly as she could, she thanked the doctor and waited for the wheelchair.

CHAPTER 15

"**Y**ou heard the doctor, Grandmother. Must you be so hardheaded?" Annie plugged in the heating pad.

"I'm not hardheaded. I heard him just fine." She hobbled to the kitchen.

"What is it you want from the kitchen, Lilly?" Patty asked, moving near her.

"A stiff drink."

"I don't think that will go well with the pain pills," Annie said.

"Oh please. I'm a tough cookie. Didn't you hear the doctor say that?" She pulled the cork of the amber liquid and poured a finger amount into her glass.

Annie watched as she tossed it back. Shaking her

head, she gazed over to Auntie Patty. "We should make some dinner."

"I'm not hungry," Lilly said, getting ready to pour another ounce of scotch.

"Grandmother. Don't." Annie's tone was enough for her to put the cork back in and slide it out of her reach.

"You're such a killjoy."

She grumbled all the way to the couch. Annie watched as she placed the now-warmed heating pad on her hip.

"I'll have Jack bring some dinner over. I have some leftovers in the fridge."

"Okay, dear. No hurry. Soon she'll be snoozing, and it will sound like a locomotive in the living room." Patty kissed Annie on the cheek.

"I don't know how you do it, Auntie. Living with her takes the patience of a saint."

"We're family, Annie. You take the bad with the good."

"Dɪᴅ you get Grandmother all settled in?" Jack was stirring some of the leftovers in a pan on the burner. The microwave beeped. Pulling open the door, he took out a sizzling plate. "I figured we'd have leftovers."

"You read my mind. Would you mind taking a couple of plates over to them? Grandmother needs some nourishment in her body. Although, between the pain pills and the scotch, she's probably already sawing logs."

He took down two plates and began dishing up the food. "Not a problem."

Annie covered the plates with foil. "Please remind her to alternate the heat with the ice."

"Will do. Back in a flash." He leaned in for a kiss.

Annie brushed her lips across his. Watching him leave, she traced her mouth with her fingers. The kiss. It was nice. It'd been a while since they'd been intimate. A warm feeling washed over her. Her man. He still had it. And she promised herself to let him know just how much.

"ALL IS WELL in the cottage. Lilly was sleeping, but she woke up and seemed to have an appetite. I set them up with the food. Patty said she'd call you before they go to bed to give you an update."

"Thank you, Jack."

They ate in silence, but the kiss they'd shared earlier played with her emotions throughout dinner, and the little butterflies she used to get when they were first a couple came fluttering back.

IT WAS JUST like old times. They tag-teamed the nightly bath routine for both children. The assembly line worked well. Jack would hand a dripping wet and giggling Ashton to Annie who'd wrap him tightly in a towel, rushing him into the bedroom. He didn't have a bashful bone in his little body, but Annie realized the importance of giving him some privacy.

"Dry off good, then put on your pajamas," Annie said, backing out of the room and closing the door almost until it clicked shut.

When she popped inside the bathroom, Jack was washing Carolina's back while she splashed water.

"I can finish her up if you want to go check on number one."

Jack moved out of the tight space, letting Annie in. She bent down at the side of the tub and began to soap up a washcloth. Could it be things were completely back to normal?

They finished the bedtime ritual, reading one of Ashton's favorite books, then both of them took their turn kissing him good night. Little Carolina was already asleep. The warm bath did it every time.

Annie took her time getting ready for bed. She washed her face with the special soap she'd treated herself to, then applied a light lotion. Normally she didn't require lotion because the humidity did a great job of keeping her skin nourished and looking youthful, but in the wintertime it never hurt to put a little bit of moisture back into the skin. Brushing her long locks until they shined, she turned off the light and entered the bedroom, expecting to see Jack asleep. He'd been sleeping a lot lately, and she wasn't sure if it was depression or something else. But there he was, wide-eyed, with a grin plastered ear to ear.

"Oh, I didn't expect you to be awake."

"I waited for you."

Kicking the covers back, she sat on the edge of the bed with her back facing him. His hand brushed her backside, sending shivers up her spine. Removing her slippers, she slowly rolled in under the sheet, resting her head on the pillow. Pulling up on his elbow, Jack studied her. She could feel his eyes all over her, and she began to blush like some newlywed.

"You're so beautiful," he said, his tone low and seductive.

She swallowed hard. The rapid pinging of her heartbeat made her feel giddy. Definitely feeling like she was experiencing something new. But this was Jack. Her husband of over six years. Someone who she'd seen through many phases of his life, the ups and the downs, the good and the bad, and he made her feel as if it were their first time as husband and wife. A warm feeling traveled through her body.

"Thank you. I don't know what I did to deserve this sort of flattery, but I like it." She moved her head and gazed at him.

He inched closer.

She studied the shape of his mouth.

He leaned in and kissed her.

When she opened her eyes, he'd moved away. "It's been a long time since you've kissed me."

"Too long." He moved back in, pushing her hair away from her face, kissing her cheek then her mouth.

It was true. It was like riding a bike. But like riding a bike with the training wheels on. Wobbly at first, a bit scared and tense you might fall but soon sailing down the sidewalk with the breeze blowing in your face, and a smile brightly lighting the way.

The love she felt for him was as big and strong, faithful, and committed as the day she said I do. And nothing they'd been through or would go through would deter her from her continued love and support.

CHAPTER 16

*L*eaning up against the counter, Annie drank the last of her coffee, trying to calm her nerves. Her first day back at the bakery, and it was leaving her a bit anxious. She was aware Jack was more than capable of taking care of the children, and with Grandmother and Auntie nearby, it comforted her even more, even though sometimes they behaved as children themselves. Shaking the last image of her elderly relatives behaving badly, she rinsed out her cup.

"You'll be fine. We'll be fine," Jack said.

She raised her brows.

"I can tell you're overthinking this going back to work thing."

She let out a long breath. "You know me so well, Jack Powell."

"Call whenever you want if it'll ease your mind," he said, slipping his hands around her waist and pulling her close.

Thank you, she mouthed.

He gave her a quick kiss before Ashton came running up behind them.

"Once he starts school in the fall, I'll feel much better about all of this." She ruffled up his hair, making him laugh.

"I'm hoping I'll be back to work by then," Jack said.

"Oh, of course. I know this is just temporary," Annie said, agreeing with him.

"I'll have dinner all ready for you when you get home. I have a therapist appointment today. Lilly and Patty are going with us. It should be very entertaining." Jack chuckled.

"I wanted to go with you," Annie said.

"Next time. There will be plenty of opportunities for you to go with me."

"I better get going. The commute traffic will be awful."

THE BELL CHIMED when Annie entered the bakery. It all felt so foreign to her. It'd been months since she'd stepped foot inside. She flicked on the lights and made her way toward the kitchen. She was early, giving her a chance to look around. Everything seemed to be in order, but the feeling of being out of place came crashing in, making her hands sweat. She put up her things, washed her hands, and slid the apron over her neck. When the bell chimed again, she saw a familiar face.

"Peter!" She rushed to him, hugging his neck.

"Annie! So good to see you again."

She let out a quick breath. Crossing her arms, she whirled around. "Everything seems the same, yet feels different." She turned back around to face him. "You know what I mean?" She shrugged.

"I do. Like you're having an out-of-body experience?" He crossed to the sink to wash his hands.

"I guess you could say that," she said.

"It'll all come back to you. It's like riding—"

"A bike," she said, finishing the sentence for him, recalling her romantic evening with Jack.

"Yes, exactly."

"So, what are we making today. And who is coming in to help us?"

Peter gave her the rundown on all the changes Sweet Indulgence had been though. When she made him manager, it was the best thing she ever did. He ran the place like it was his own. They'd lost some good employees over the course of the year or two. Rebecca worked at her family's restaurant the Black-Eyed Pea, Morgan went on to graduate school and left South Carolina, and when Betsy and Charles tied the knot, they retired and were traveling the globe.

"What about Toby and Keith?" Annie asked. She had to admit, she was hoping to see her favorite twins.

"What can I say about the duo. They got girlfriends, and soon they were working less and less."

"I cannot figure that out. When a guy gets a girl-friend, they need money. Why work less?" Annie asked.

"I have no clue. I guess that's why I'm single. Right now, I'm the only full-time employee," Peter said as he moved to the cabinets.

"I remember those days," she said, helping him retrieve the dry ingredients.

"I have two college students who work four hours each, four days a week."

"That doesn't give you much time off."

"I don't have much of a social life. It's all good."

"Put me on the schedule for five hours Monday through Friday to start. I need the weekends off."

"Are you sure? You're just coming back. Maybe take it slow. And it's the busiest time of the year for us— besides Valentine's."

"Okay. How about four?" she said, acknowledging she may be a bit eager.

"Sounds good. And if I need you in a pinch, I'll see if you can work more. By the way, how is Jack doing?" He lifted a large bag of flour and put it up on the stainless counter.

"He's doing great. I'm very happy with his progress. He still has a way to go, but he's being much more positive, so I'm hopeful. Thanks for asking."

"Do you think he'll be back in the wood design business again?"

"He wants to, but I just don't know."

"Many people with far more disability go on to accomplish so much. I wouldn't count it out."

"I don't disagree with you at all. I hope it's just temporary, and he gets back doing what he loves. I know it's important to feel useful and do something you love." The volume in her tone dropped as she spoke the words, wishing she could take a few of them back. They were too revealing.

"Hey, is that regret I hear in your voice?" Peter laughed it off and went to work adding ingredients into the powerful mixers.

"I love being Ashton and Carolina's mom and Jack's wife. It's the best thing that ever happened to me. Besides Sweet Indulgence."

"I know this was your baby," he said, not looking at her while he worked.

"Yes, but even babies are put to bed, eventually." She lifted her shoulders.

"We're making chocolate, vanilla, and spice today." He pushed over the recipe card for her to read.

"Ahh! Some of my favorites are still going strong. Caramel sea salt, Black Forest, and cream cheese frostings." She winked.

"It's the holidays. We'll be adding a bunch in over the next couple of weeks."

"Oh, that reminds me. We're having a get-together over at the house on the twenty-fourth. Please come."

"You're planning a party and going back to work. You're a brave soul."

"Actually, Jack is planning it. It's giving him something to do. We went and picked out the tree last week. Of course, it was with incident." She followed along the recipe card with her finger, then searched the table for the baking soda.

"What sort of incident?" Peter asked.

"Grandmother face-planted with a tree."

"Is she all right?"

"Yes. Just a hurt ego and a bruised hip."

"Hate to end the chitchat, but we have cupcakes to

bake. They should be cooled and ready to ice by the time Chrissy gets here."

"Chrissy?"

"She's a College of Charleston student. So far, she's been very reliable."

THEY WORKED the next couple of hours mixing up batter, filling cupcake pans, and baking. The aroma of warm, delightful treats wafted through the kitchen, making the fond memories of how it all started surface. Peter insisted she take a break and put her feet up. She didn't argue with him. Her dogs were barking and barking loudly. She wandered over to a table in the corner, bringing her lunch Jack had prepared. How they'd reversed roles amazed her. And so quickly. She nibbled on the cheese and crackers and celery sticks and washed it down with water. A few people trickled in, purchasing cupcakes prominently displayed, and she overheard Peter taking a special order too. When a blonde girl came bouncing through the door, Annie thought she was a customer until she headed around the counter to the kitchen. She could hear Peter and the girl chatting. Must be Chrissy, she assumed. Gathering up her lunch and moving toward the laughter, she stood in the doorway and waited for her introduction.

While Chrissy iced the cupcakes, Peter took his much-earned break. Annie took that moment to tell him something he had to have known all along.

"She's a cutie, and she likes you."

"What?" He looked over Annie's shoulder toward Chrissy.

"Yes. Trust me. And if you don't want to mess it up, you best do a better job at learning women's hints and flirts. 'Cuz she, my friend, was flirting big time." Annie patted his arm.

Shaking his head, he looked down at the ground. "I don't have a lot of experience."

"And some girls like that. Just sayin'…"

"Annie. You're making me blush," he said.

"And some girls like that too." She slapped him on the back. "Go get 'em, tiger."

THANK GOODNESS FOR CRUISE CONTROL. Exhausted, Annie headed home after her first day back after being gone for over two years. Oh sure, she'd kept an eye on the financial side of the business, but even then, she let Peter make hiring and firing decisions. Being a silent partner had its perks, but she did enjoy rolling up her sleeves and getting back to work.

The kids were so excited to see her, she could barely get inside the house before the squealing began, followed by all-out laughter. Jack stood back with arms crossed, smiling.

"How was your first day?"

"Great. I'm tired, but it was so nice to see the place and be a part of it again."

"Dinner is ready. Why don't you get into something comfortable and come join us?" He moved toward the kitchen.

"It smells divine," she said as she traveled down the hall, both kids in tow.

Plates heaping with spaghetti and meatballs sat waiting for her. He even remembered the wine.

"Jack, you outdid yourself." She pulled out a chair and sat.

"After my appointment, we went shopping. Lilly and Patty helped me, and I think I got everything for the party."

"You've been quite busy too." She dug into the pasta and swirled it on her fork.

"We got the tree," Ashton said in between slurps of pasta.

Annie looked over to the corner where they always placed the Christmas tree. Turning back around, she beamed. "Yeah. Now we can decorate it."

"We'll do it tomorrow. You eat and relax," Jack said.

"But I love to decorate the tree and house for the holidays," she said, her tone dropping a few levels, showing her disappointment.

"Is the bakery open on Christmas Eve?"

"You know I didn't ask. I did invite Peter to the party. He didn't say anything about the shop's hours."

"Well, as the boss, you could close it for the day. I'm sure the employees would love a day off."

"True, but if memory serves me, Christmas Eve is a busy time. People are buying last-minute dessert items for the holiday and also for gift giving."

"Ask Peter tomorrow, and then let me know the game plan. Lilly and Patty are standing by to help me make all the food."

"What sort of things are you having?" It felt strange to ask Jack this question. She'd always been the planner.

"Chips and salsa, veggie tray and dip, chicken wings, chili...and I'm forgetting something else—oh and cheese and crackers. Gotta have cheese and crackers with our wine." He winked.

"Sounds good. What about some dry salami? That goes well with the cheese and crackers," she said.

"Got it. I guess I was forgetting a couple of things. We also got stuff to make cookies. The kids and I are going to do that tomorrow and the next day. With Lilly and Patty's help, of course."

Annie sat back. Everything was going so well. Isn't that what she wanted? For Jack to be productive, feel useful, and let her go back to work while he healed?

Then why did she feel so left out?

CHAPTER 17

*E*ach day at the bakery, Annie gave one hundred percent. Each night, Jack gave one hundred percent. At least in her mind he was giving more. As he got into the routine, not only did he have dinner ready, but the house was clean, the laundry done, oh, and the house was decorated for Christmas. Granted, he didn't have her crafty touch to decorating, but he definitely got an A for effort.

"Jack, honey. You're doing so much. You must be as tired as I am. Maybe even more so." With her eyelids hooding over her eyes, she tasted the homemade chili.

"I'm keeping busy, and that's a good thing. The therapist—"

Annie's eyes flew open. "Jack...you were supposed

to tell me when the next appointment was." She set her spoon down, giving him a scornful look.

"First of all, stop throwing the daggers at me. It's okay that you're not accompanying me to them."

"I want to show I'm supportive," she said, pouting.

"You are supportive." He slid out his chair and came around to her side of the table.

"I feel like everything has changed. I'm on a merry-go-round and can't get off." She lowered her gaze.

Lifting her chin with his finger, he tilted her head, his eyes never wavering from hers. "I feel like that some-times, too, but we're making it work. We have a great support system here. The operative word being system. Lilly, Patty, Mary, Mom and Dad, everyone. They're here to help us."

"I know they are. It's just that I'm usually the one helping."

"Stop the pity party right now, Annie Powell. I'm the one who was injured." His loving tone turned harsh.

Man, did those words hit her in the head like a brick. He was right. So what if her little consistent world had changed. His changed in ways she'd never know. *Get a grip, Annie*, she could hear Grandmother say. Life isn't fair, she'd say. A tear bobbled on her bottom lid, eventu-ally dropping down her cheek.

"I'm sorry, Jack. You're right. I'm feeling sorry for

myself, and that's not cool. From now on, there'll be no more pity parties here. Only the best Christmas Eve celebration ever." She leaped to her feet and wrapped her arms around his neck. Leaning back so she could see all of his face, she paused. Saving the best for last was something she loved doing.

"Jack, you keep me grounded. I can't imagine my life without you or the children. You've given us a beautiful home and a wonderful life. I love you." She moved her lips to his, pressing softly at first, then with more emotion, setting another kiss for the records.

"Mommy and Daddy are kissing," Ashton sang out.

While still holding on to the last seconds of the kiss, Annie and Jack started chuckling. Pulling back, he kissed her nose then rushed over to Ashton.

"Yes, Daddy was kissing Mommy. Her lips taste yummy." He looked up and winked at Annie.

And just like that, they went from down in the dumps to flying high. A roller coaster, a merry-go-round, whatever you wanted to name it. Life was full of ups and downs, and the Powells were no different. But if Annie knew one thing for sure, they'd recover from all the lows, and soon, sunny days with blue skies would be their mantra. Forever.

The kids had saved a few ornaments for Annie to place on the tree. The tree they'd picked up while she was at work. The one they'd found before Grandmother had her little accident. She was surprised to find out it was still there. Jack later confided that he'd hid it among some trees, making it difficult to see. In all of the commotion of Grandmother's accident, she didn't even realize he'd done that.

A few of the plastic containers were still packed with holiday decorations. Annie chose a few and set them around. It made her feel like part of the celebration. And even with the sorest feet, she stood at the counter and made cookies with Ashton. Wasn't that being a parent? You roll up your sleeves, make a cup of coffee, and you dig in, doing what is important for the child. It built memories, and Annie was all about that, recalling the time capsule she and Jack buried near the magnolia tree.

After the kitchen was closed for the night and the kids were snuggled in their beds, Jack and Annie snuggled on the couch.

"I love Christmastime, especially with the children," she said, leaning back into his arm.

"Yup. It's the best." He reached his left arm around her.

Reaching down, she rested her hand on his stub, feeling the ace bandage under her fingertips.

"Everything is ready for the big party, except for the

wood," he said, staring straight ahead at the flickering flames in the fireplace.

"I'm going to help with that tomorrow. I'll get Grandmother to keep an eye on the kids."

"I have Danny and Mary coming tomorrow. While he and I chop, she's going to watch the kids."

"Oh," she said tersely.

"Annie," he sang, giving her the look.

"No, I'm not jealous. I'm glad they're helping you." Turning, she faced him. "I may just be a tad bit jealous." She held her fingers apart, showing him. "But then I quickly dismissed it. This is good. This is good." She leaned back into his arms.

He played with the ends of her hair. "Good because family is part of our support system. Just repeat after me." He chuckled.

Annie playfully slapped his leg. "Yes, Jack, I got it."

"But just so you don't feel completely left out, I will need some help with the food. I think it's too much on Lilly and Patty, after all."

"Do you think they're feeling all right?"

"I think so. It's their age, Annie. It's creeping up on them. They get winded easily, take longer naps, aren't eating quite as much as they used to. It's all about the slowing down process of the elderly. It's happening with my grandparents too. They're coming to the party, but I bet all of them will be napping in the cottage before the night is through." He let out a snicker.

"I probably should make a doctor appointment for them," Annie said.

"After the holidays. They wouldn't want anything to spoil the children's festivities."

"So, you do think something is wrong. Have they shared anything with you?" Annie said, verbalizing her concern.

"Not in so many words. Just the observation I've made. I think it's just old age."

"Just the same, I think I'll make an appointment for them. It's been a while since they've been seen."

"What do you mean? Lilly was just seen in the ER."

"Ha ha, Jack."

"I'm glad you're able to see the humor in things. No matter what life throws at us, we must still laugh," he said.

"That's sound advice. I'll definitely try to remember that."

Jack took off to check on the children, leaving her alone with her thoughts. Propping her feet up on the coffee table, she fell into a slumber.

Opening her eyes wide, she sat up. "What?" She knitted her brows together.

"You were talking in your sleep."

Annie shifted her gaze away. Now she remembered. She was dreaming of their date on the boat, and how they'd gotten caught in a summer downpour. Seemed like a lifetime ago.

"I guess I dozed off. Do you remember our first date on the boat?"

"How could I forget. You were so beautiful. We had a nice dinner, and then it rained on us when we got back to the dock."

"And we ran laughing to the car. Soaked, but so unbelievably happy," she said, smiling.

"I'm glad you're still regarding our courtship as happy times," he said.

"Jack, everything about us are happy times. I love you with all of my heart."

"I know you do. And I love you too. Why do you suppose we're going down memory lane tonight?"

"I don't know. I guess we've been through so much over the last several years. It's good to reminisce about the good old days."

He drew her hand in his and urged her to stand. An all too familiar moment settled in between them. He leaned in. She inched closer. She posed for the kiss.

A shrill cry came from Carolina's bedroom, breaking the enchantment. Annie rushed down the hall, and Jack was right behind her.

CHAPTER 18

*B*racing her hands against Carolina's doorframe, her gaze floated from the empty crib to the floor. There, lying on the floor, was a sobbing Carolina. She hurried to her, cradling Carolina in her arms. She looked her over for any obvious signs of injury. A red spot on her forehead concerned her.

"Oh, baby girl, did you fall out of your crib?" She kissed the spot on her forehead.

"I think we have a little tomboy on our hands. She climbed over the railing," Jack said.

"I think so. She's learning a lot from Ashton," Annie said, studying the small goose egg on Carolina's forehead. "She's going to have quite a bump here. Let's get some ice on it," she said, following Jack to the kitchen.

"Is it my imagination, or do children interfere with

their parents' love life?" Jack opened the freezer and put some cubes in a baggie.

Taking the baggie, Annie wrapped it in a tea towel from the kitchen drawer and gently held it in place on Carolina's head. "It seems like it."

"I think she'll survive the fall, don't you?" Jack said.

"Just to be sure, I'm going to keep her awake for a bit. We know she hit her head. Go on to bed. I'll be there eventually."

"Annie, we're in this together, remember? Besides, it's still early." He winked.

WITH ANOTHER EMERGENCY AVERTED, Annie breathed a sigh of relief as she finally settled into bed with a sleeping Jack at her side. It was time to put all the craziness behind them and prepare for their holiday celebration. Who was she kidding? All the Powell and McPherson gatherings had some form of craziness. That's what made them so much fun.

EVERYONE LOVED A GOOD PARTY, and Annie and Jack were known to throw some of the best. And despite living on the tiny island, and a drive for most people, few people declined their invitation. The weather cooperated beyond anyone's wildest wishes. A light chill in the air made it perfect for the bonfire, and the clear night sky lit up with stars added to the glorious evening under the deeply wooded lot Sweet Magnolia shared. Jack had installed lighting the summer before, and with the strings of mason jar lights around the gazebo, trellis, and on limbs of trees, the grounds sparkled like fairy dust.

Danny stacked the wood inside the large, rocked pit and lit it, getting it started before everyone showed up. Mary, Annie, Grandmother, and Patty were putting the finishing touches on the appetizers and drinks. Jack gathered the chairs and sat them around the pit. Annie couldn't help but check on the men every so often. Her chest puffed out when she saw Jack lifting chairs, moving tables around, and doing all the things he used to do prepping for parties.

"Jack seems to be doing well," Mary said as she sliced the salami.

"He is. It was rough for a while," Annie said.

"He's going to therapy more, and it shows," Patty said, gleaming ear to ear.

"I don't know what all the fuss is about. Jack Powell always knew what he had to do to cope with this tragedy.

It just took him a bit to get there. Therapists, poo," Lilly said, pouring her second glass of wine.

"Grandmother, therapists are wonderful professionals. They help many people."

"Yeah, Grandmother. They help Danny all the time with his PTSD," Mary said.

Grandmother waved them off and sat. "Medical professionals are all the same. They take your money, and all they can do is guess about stuff. No two people are the same. What works for one may not work for others."

"Well, I'm glad you have such a high opinion of them because I've made you and Auntie doctor appointments."

"What?" Lilly sat her wineglass down hard.

"Yes. It's been well over a year since you saw your doctor."

"I just saw a doctor a couple of weeks ago," she argued.

"That was an emergency room doctor. He was checking you just for your hip. He also said we needed to follow up with your primary doctor. I would hate for anyone to think I don't take care of you, and report me." Annie sliced cheese.

Sighing deeply and loudly for everyone to hear, Grandmother picked up her glass. "I suppose so. If memory serves me, my doctor was pretty handsome."

The ladies all broke out laughing.

"Go ahead and laugh," Lilly said. "But I read somewhere that the libido doesn't die until you're in the ground."

Patty gasped, covering her mouth to hide her giggles. Mary shook her head. Annie, cocking her head with her hands on her hips, said, "You're so incorrigible sometimes."

"But you love me, right?" She winked.

"Always," Annie said.

ANNIE'S EYES lit up when Vicky and Scott walked in the door with Jasmine and her baby brother, Jackson. Annie held out her arms, nuzzling little Jackson's soft face.

"He's precious," Annie said.

"We're all adjusting. Jasmine has been such a big help to Mommy." Vicky ran her fingers through the little girl's curls.

Vicky had taken to motherhood. Jasmine's hair was done up with the prettiest red bows, she had on a cute Christmas outfit, and Jackson's jet-black hair, what little he had, was neatly combed. He, too, was dressed in a festive outfit.

"I've wanted to visit so many times. It's just been a bit chaotic over here," Annie said.

Scott waved off Annie's words. "No worries. We know you two have had your share of stuff. We were just waiting for the right time."

"There's no time like a Christmas shindig at the Powell's," Mary said, breaking up the little happy reunion.

"Hi, Mary," Vicky said.

"Look at you. The happy little family. We're all so glad you could come today. We need some joy, don't we?" Mary tickled Jackson's tummy, making him giggle.

"We're good at spreading joy," Scott said.

They all looked up when they heard more laughter.

"Oh my. Look who just crashed our party!" Annie ran over and hugged Cassie, her friend from college who she'd not seen in ages.

"Annie, you look great," Cassie said.

"This can't be little Katy!" Annie leaned over and smiled at the little girl who wasn't a toddler anymore.

"Yes. Hasn't she grown?" Cassie's gaze dropped to her daughter.

They got out all the hugs and wiped away the tears of happiness when the next set of guests arrived. And before too long, they were joined by another college friend, Jessica and her husband, Tom, and their son Reece. But it was only when Dr. Michael Carlisle and Rebecca came waltzing in with their precious daughter, Kathryn, that the circle of friends was complete. Everyone else who came after, except Charles and Betsy, were family by blood. But this special group of people was just as much family. They didn't get to see them as often, but when they did, it was like old home week.

The spread that the ladies put out had the group complimenting them. Annie could never take full credit, so she made sure those who did the good deed got their due. And at nightfall, Jack and Danny created one massive fire, flames shooting high into the dark sky. Everybody bundled up as they sat around the roaring fire, feeling the warmth radiating around them. The children roasted marshmallows while the adults reminisced. Every now and then, Grandmother and Auntie would interject and get a laugh out of them. Robert and Milly Powell were more stoic, but once Milly had a couple of glasses of wine, she opened up. Jack's sister and her family came. It was nice to have family and friends help them celebrate so many great things. Even Jack's grandparents on both sides came, although soon, all the old folks headed back to the cottage for a game of cards and real warmth.

Letting out a deep breath, Annie stared up into the sky. So many stars were out on this cold evening. A night where you could see your breath, and no matter how many layers, the chill could be felt to the bone. She drew her lap blanket up to cover Carolina, swaddling her tightly.

"It's getting a tad cold out here for the children. Maybe we should take the party back inside?"

While Jack and all the men stayed back to make sure the fire was out, the women and children entered Sweet Magnolia. She switched on the gas fireplace and told everyone to make themselves comfortable. She put Carolina to bed but allowed Ashton to stay up to play with his "friends," as he called them. The other moms got the kids interested in some games, then helped themselves to another glass of wine while they waited for the men.

"I'm so glad Jack is doing well," Rebecca said.

"Yes, me too. It's been a tough hill to climb, but I think we're on the downward hike," Annie said.

"I know we're all so darn busy, but we need to set aside time to get together once in a while," Cassie said.

"I'm back at work. For the time being anyway. At least until Jack figures out what he wants to do. Stop by someday, and we can have lunch. It's not just a bakery anymore." Annie tipped her head and shrugged.

"Oh, we know. We've stopped in many times while Peter was running the place. He's done such a great job. He could use more help, though. Sometimes the wait is a tad too long. I worried you may be losing customers," Rebecca said.

Annie knew full well that Rebecca had experience with this topic. She was running a restaurant herself. The Black-Eyed Pea was a favorite of Grandmother and Auntie's.

"I know. I think I'll try to hire some more folks to help us. I just want to work part-time."

"I'm sure you'll find someone," Diane, Jack's sister, said.

"I'd ask my sister to help out, but then you'd be short an employee," Annie said, smirking at Mary.

"I'm happy to help you out on the weekends, Sis. Just say the word."

"I might just take you up on that offer."

The door flew open, letting a whoosh of cold air in. The men all trampled inside, taking care to wipe their feet first. Isla and Buffy ran up with their tails wagging.

"I remember when she was just a pup," Ryan said, patting Isla on the head.

"And I remember when Buffy was too," Cassie said, scratching Buffy under her chin.

"She's getting up there. I guess none of us stay young forever," Annie said.

"No, but we can sure as heck try. I'm not giving up on youth," Mary said.

"Grandmother always says you're only as old as you feel," Annie said.

"Well, in that case, she's going to outlive us all!" Mary said.

The entire room fell out laughing.

The group stuck around for a bit longer, then one by one the couples left, leaving Jack and Annie standing in the middle of the once boisterous room, now quiet, and dimly lit by the gas fireplace.

"We did it again," Jack said, holding her hand.

"It was a great party. I loved seeing all the smiling faces and everyone catching up. It warms my heart," she said.

"And what about those old folks? If I ever start to count any of that bunch out, holler at me," Jack said, picking up the clutter around the room.

"Leave that, Jack. We can clean up tomorrow. I'm bushed. Let's call it a night." She flexed her arm outward and opened her hand.

He moved toward her, taking her hand, he clasped it tightly. "I've been thinking a lot tonight about my situation," he said as they walked toward the bedroom.

"Oh?" She furrowed her brows.

"I'm going to open up the woodshop again. Not until after the new year though."

"Are you sure?"

"I'm sure. I'll start off slow, see how I do, but the therapist said if I have the desire, I should at least try."

"And do you? Have the desire?"

"I do. I dream about it during all hours of the day. I want to get back into it. I need to for my sanity."

"I'll support you in any way I can, Jack. You do know that, right?"

"Of course. That's why we make such a great team. I can read your mind, you can finish my sentences, and we're just like one." He pulled her close.

"Well, if that's true, what am I thinking?" Annie batted her lashes while giving him a sexy look, while teasingly playing with her hair.

Leaning in, he brushed his mouth across hers. "How's that for mind reading?"

"I like it. I like it a lot, Mr. Powell." She looped her hands around his neck and pulled him in for another.

EPILOGUE

*A*nnie and Jack went through a few more ups and downs, but once they smoothed out, it was like riding in Lady Powell on calm waters. Perfect. In the fall, Ashton started school, and Carolina, like Ashton before her, played at Grandmother Milly's while Mommy and Daddy went to work. Annie started off working only part-time, but after she'd been there for a few months, she couldn't fathom not being there full-time. Jack slowly went back to work at Powell's Sweet Wood Design. He only took basic orders at first, eventually graduating to more complex items. Grandmother and Auntie were still hanging on, but Annie prepared herself for the day they'd be gone. Whenever one of them got ill or had to start taking a new medication, she wondered if their end was nearing. The one consistent thing they did was Sunday dinner, and even on the days when Grandmother wasn't feeling particularly well, she came dressed in coordinated apparel. And during the spring and early summer, before it got too hot, both Grandmother and Auntie pleaded with Jack for boat rides on Lady Powell. They didn't have to plead too hard, but it was fun to see them do their best to convince him why he should take them.

"It will probably be our last boat ride," Lilly said, crying crocodile tears.

"Yeah, Jack. Do it for us. Do it for one last time," Patty said in her most dramatic tone.

Jack held up his hand. "No worries. Grab your shawls, grab your sunbonnets. Lady Powell leaves the dock in five minutes."

"What?" Lilly grabbed Patty's hand, tugging her to the front door.

"Don't leave without us," Lilly called out as they hit the porch running.

"Jack," Annie said, trying to hide her giggles.

"See how fast they took off to the cottage? Those two aren't even close to calling it a day."

"I know, but I can't afford to have them get hurt. Grandmother might sprain an ankle or something."

Jack widened his eyes. He rushed to the door and

opened it. "Lilly. Patty. Wait up." He tore out of the house, leaving Annie alone. Shaking her head, the corners of her mouth drew up.

Jack continued with therapy and got on a list for a prosthesis. Annie realized it would mean Jack had to learn how to use it, and with that challenge, would come more anguish. But she prepared for it, too, like she prepared for the day Grandmother and Patty would leave.

Mary and Danny stayed on at the old Charleston homestead. After all of her complaining, she decided it wasn't so bad after all. And soon, they had their own little one crawling around, giving everyone something else to be grateful for.

The college friends made a pact and stuck with it to see each other more often. Sometimes it was just a quick lunch, sometimes it was a girls' night out, just like old times. Annie loved seeing them, and even though they'd gone in different directions, they found time to stay connected, and it made her happy.

Vicky, Scott, Jasmine, and Jackson visited often, and on many summer days you could find them down at their little slice of heaven, the private beaches they shared on the tiny island, basking in the sun, watching the children play, throwing back a few cold ones and remembering the good times.

Annie and Jack had a lot to be grateful for, and they vowed never to take anything they had for granted, including each other.

ABOUT THE AUTHOR

A USA Today bestselling author, Debbie writes sweet contemporary romance and women's fiction. She lives in South Carolina with her husband and two dachshund rescues, Dash and Briar. An avid supporter of animal rescue, Debbie happily donates a percentage of all book sales to local and national rescue organizations. When you purchase any of her books, you're also helping animals.

To find out more about Debbie, check out her website at https://www.authordebbiewhite.com

BOOKS BY DEBBIE WHITE

Romance Across State Lines

Texas Twosome

Kansas Kissed

California Crush

Oregon Obsession

Florida Fling

Montana Miracle

Pennsylvania Passion

Romantic Destinations

Finding Mrs. Right

Holding on to Mrs. Right

Cherishing Mrs. Right

Charleston Harbor Novels

Sweet Indulgence

Sweet Magnolia

Sweet Carolina

Sweet Remembrance

Stand Alone Books

Perfect Pitch

Ties That Bind

Passport To Happiness

The Missing Ingredient

The Salty Dog

The Pet Palace

Billionaire Auction

Billionaire's Dilemma

Coaching the Sub

Christmas Romance – Short Stories